Trey's Company

Trey's Company

Frank Murtaugh

Mojo Triangle Books™
An Imprint Of

A traditional publisher
with a non-traditional approach to publishing

Library of Congress Control Number: 2017937354
ISBN: 978-1-941644-85-0

Sartoris Literary Group, Inc.
Jackson, Mississippi
www.sartorisliterary.com

For Sofia and Elena

Remember who you are

Prologue

The sirens changed everything. At first a mild distraction . . . somewhere in the distance. Then gradually louder, approaching.

You didn't hear sirens in Cleveland, Tennessee. Ever. Not on Friday night. Not on any night.

Libby was already in bed. Gran had her feet up on the couch. Me, I had one leg dangling over the arm of Granddaddy's lounge chair. *Dallas* had been on 10 minutes, maybe 15. That made it around 9:15 that Friday night.

I wasn't looking forward to the flight home four days from now. Back to Mom and Dad. Back to school. Two thousand miles away from my grandmother, from my summer oasis in east Tennessee. I hadn't been sulking through *The Dukes of Hazzard* and the first few confrontations on *Dallas*. But I'd been silent. Then the sirens.

As they neared Gran's house, their wail began to pierce not only the silence, but my thoughts. *Woo-woo-woo-woo-woo.* I sure as hell didn't care what Bobby Ewing had to say anymore.

I felt my heart rate climb as the police cruisers — two of them, one behind the other — drove directly past Gran's house. This wasn't normal. I looked at Gran. She'd straightened up on the couch, lowering her legs to the floor.

No one was speeding down Westview Drive. Even if some careless teenager had been, no way are two police cruisers dispatched for the chase.

Before the sirens were out of earshot . . . another siren. Coming from the same direction as the police cars. But a different sound this time. A different wail. *Weeee-ooooo . . . weeee-ooooo . . . weeee-ooooo.*

An ambulance. Thirteen years were enough life to know the difference between a police siren and that of an ambulance. Again, the siren grew louder as it neared, then passed directly in front of Gran's house. Following the path of those police cruisers.

My palms were now damp. And Gran's brow furrowed in a way it seldom did until this summer. She was worried, which made me worry. She was scared, which made me . . . .

Wendy. I stood out of the chair as the hair on the back of my neck tingled. Those sirens were moving toward Wendy's house. God, let them move past Wendy's house. Way past Wendy's house.

I didn't bother to find shoes (or socks). As I sprinted out Gran's front door into the darkness, I heard her shout behind me . . . "Trey!"

1

Memories may blur, but not from the summer of 1982. Every summer was great, but the memories of that one summer at Gran's seem to tickle my thoughts more than others. Mom and Dad were 2,000 miles away, which may as well have been the moon to a thirteen-year-old's sense of proportion. My sister was there, too. She was old enough to know when to leave me alone, but young enough to get in the way.

Didn't matter. It was the best summer ever. I played baseball — by myself, but in front of millions. I fell in love . . . at least what I thought love was. And I very nearly burned down an entire subdivision of new homes. But that didn't matter, either.

It was the best summer ever. In many ways, it was my *last* summer.

The South is where summers should be spent. They're hot down here, *sweaty*. Beaches are for vacation, New England for winters, the Midwest for farming. The South is for summers, and my parents knew this.

Mom and Dad were what they liked to call "academic gypsies," working toward their Ph.D.'s —

Dad's in economics, Mom's in history — well into their thirties. Learning was their career in my eyes, and it rubbed off. That curiosity. Our home in southern California had far more books than silverware. Questions were treated like the finest dessert, something to be not only chewed upon, but fully savored before swallowing. The academic year went by quicker for my family than for most.

But when summer arrived, when a child's formal learning takes a brilliant three-month pause (during which so much more is actually learned), Mom and Dad shipped my sister and me back east, to Cleveland, Tennessee, where my maternal grandmother — Gran we called her — lived with a pair of Boston Terriers. Bootsie and Buster were decent company, but Gran often told us her house "came alive" when Libby and I arrived in June.

Cleveland is too small to call a city, but too big to deserve the romanticized tag of Southern town. It's a bedroom community, really, about 30 miles northeast of Chattanooga, 80 miles southwest of Knoxville. What it had to offer — in 1982 at least — wasn't industry, but comfort. Roses was the department store, which anchored a garden-variety mall. There were two movie theatres in town, each with a pair of screens. A two-mile "strip" had the requisite fast-food chains, with a family-owned diner at either end.

And that was it.

People didn't come to Cleveland as a destination, but as a home, a place to rest. As Gran put it, you could "while the hours away" here and no one would "pay it any mind." No sirens, so no emergencies. When the sun went down, so did the people. Perhaps it would have been too quiet for me in a few years, but just out of 7th grade, with the playground of my own imagination to help me "while away the hours and days" . . . it was paradise.

Gran's house — at 343 Westview Drive — was in a neighborhood a comfortable distance from the interstate. It was a one-story brick "ranch" home, though I never quite got the description. It had a carport with a mysterious utility shed that seemed ominous before I knew what the word meant. A pair of magnolia trees towered over Gran's front yard, hiding much of the house from passersby.

One of those magnolias was directly in front of my room, the first of three bedrooms as you wandered down the hallway after passing through what Gran called "the living quarters." Libby stayed in the back room on the left, just across the hallway from Gran's room. (It was Granddaddy's too, of course, but he died a year before we started spending summers with Gran. You'll hear plenty about him though.) I used to wonder if Gran's house was big enough for her, as you could hear Bootsie whimper from one end to the other when she needed to go outside. Or maybe the house was too big for her since she started living alone. "It just fits," she'd tell me. She smiled when she did.

* * *

By the way, my name is Charles Michael Milligan III. I liked my name then, and I like it now. I actually gained a reputation in preschool for introducing myself without skipping a solitary syllable.

"Hi there, young man. I'm Ms. Jefferson."

"Hello. I'm Charles Michael Milligan III."

"Hey, I'm Tommy."

"Howdy. I'm Charles Michael Milligan III."

I've never answered to the name Charlie. Don't plan on it. But you can call me Trey.

* * *

My grandmother Johnson was the youngest of eleven kids in her family. She blamed the timing of her birth on her given names: Will Cooper. "Mama and Daddy just ran out of names," she'd say, not always smiling at the notion. "At least they ran out of girls' names."

But Gran was very much a lady. She dressed casually — I remember the polyester slacks most clearly — but with a sense of comfortable style. Her hair was kept short, dyed a shade I could only describe as golden. (It actually shone in sunlight.)

There are two parts of a human face that never age: the eyes and smile. Now, Gran had her share of wrinkles at the side of her eyes — crow's feet I was taught to call them — and a few around her mouth, as she smoked more than she should have. But she had the eyes of a schoolgirl, and her smile filled a room, especially when she was doting on Libby and me.

"You know, Trey, your blue eyes and brown hair are God's way of showing He loves you . . . but I'm here to prove it." Gran reminded me of this every summer, as though I'd never heard it before. Also, "I love you a bushel and a peck, and then some." Having grown up a city mouse, I took the quantity to be immeasurable . . . sure felt like it.

Gran made the summer ours once Libby and I arrived. The only real discipline I remember came when I was cruel to my little sister. Five years younger, Libby had her own agenda. A few dolls, her own books ("Little Prouse on the Harry" finally began to make sense when she turned 8), and two dogs that couldn't get enough attention. She mingled

13

with Gran, crossed my path a few times for snacks and meals, and left a boy's world to the boy of the house. The three of us — us humans — made a good team.

I learned the word *humid* during my summers in east Tennessee. Playing outside in Cleveland in June was like swimming without the splash. It was less hot than it was sticky. "Swampy" would be a good way to describe it. But it was always baseball weather to me.

* * *

"I'm playing ball, Gran."

Didn't wait for a reply as I slid open and quickly closed the sliding-glass door to Gran's backyard ballfield. I've been to Yankee Stadium in New York, Fenway Park in Boston, Dodger Stadium in L.A., and two Busch Stadiums in St. Louis, but no field will ever compare to the contorted, constricted, fenced diamond where I won the '82 pennant for St. Louis — by myself, mind you — two months before the Cardinals actually did so themselves a short drive south in Atlanta.

To enter the backyard, you first stepped onto a patio, raised four feet, edged in brick and covered with, yes, Astroturf. Gran didn't know what that fake grass meant in the eyes of a baseball fan, only that it prevented her from slipping in the rain. But it was an emerald mood-setter of the first order for a boy on his way to a big-league mound someday.

That "mound" — the worn patch of dirt I had permanently etched into Gran's yard — was forty feet from that four-foot brick wall that supported the patio. And it was against that wall where I hurled a rubber ball — solid, heavier than a racquetball but smaller than a baseball — all summer long.

I was the Cardinals — all of them, the whole roster — in that backyard. Fitted hat, securely on my head; bill pulled low on my brow. My opponent was whomever St. Louis was next scheduled to play. If it was the Phillies, I had to deal with Mike Schmidt and Pete Rose. Steve Garvey and Dusty Baker dug into my imagination's batter's box on days when the Dodgers were on the schedule. I kept score, and I didn't always win. But I played my hardest, every morning, every afternoon. The small pear tree to my left was second base, the thicker maple to my right was third. First base? That was a throwback to the brick "backstop" after fielding the rebound of a pitch.

When I managed to hit the corner of the wall, where the patio ended and the wall began — wrapped in that faux turf — the ball would fly upward toward me. And when I hit that precise height hard enough, the ball might just fly over the chain-link fence behind me. When the Cardinals were batting (and that's the only time I ever aimed for that corner), I witnessed some of the prettiest sixty-foot home runs a boy will ever see. Sure made hopping the fence a happy skill to learn.

Gran left me alone in my field of dreams. Libby too. The only time either would interrupt me would be when a visitor stopped by. And there were only two visitors in Gran's neighborhood.

2

"Traaa-ay . . . Larrrr-ry's here!"

Libby had her own way of shouting my name, adding a syllable and a sing-song pattern to what was otherwise a fairly simple expression. She did the same thing in announcing Larry Blackwell's numerous arrivals at Gran's front door. Though the way she "sang" Larrr-ry was more mocking than tribute.

Before meeting Larry Blackwell Jr., you need to know his father. And you need to know what Gran thought of L. Roy Blackwell, Esquire.

Mr. Blackwell was the senior partner at Blackwell, Brownstone, and Crowley, a law firm in Chattanooga that specialized in "protecting the injured or overlooked." He was tall, but with slumped shoulders. Mr. Blackwell combed his jet-black hair with what Gran described as a "mechanic's fistful of grease." But that hair was never — ever — out of place. Not even on Sunday morning when, like Gran, the Blackwell family was in church only "in spirit."

Gran warned me the first time I was allowed to visit Larry's house without her supervision. "The

Blackwells are nice folks," she said. I knew that Gran would deliver an insult sandwiched between a pair of compliments. "But you just cannot trust a lawyer you see on billboards. Now Crystal [that was Larry's mom], she can prepare a quiche that will make you forget you ever had one before."

Everyone in Cleveland knew Mr. Blackwell's first name was Lawrence. And it was considered "high falutin'" that he chose to use the initial of his first name before his middle name on every last one of those billboards, or newspaper ads, or posters at the bus station. But Gran got a kick out of always calling him "L. Roy," even to his face. Gran knew Mr. Blackwell didn't exactly like the two-names-as-one delivery, but she also knew he couldn't exactly protest, as such was precisely the way he presented his name to every potential client in east Tennessee. "Good afternoon, L. Roy," Gran would say as she greeted him at the door. "When's Crystal gonna bring me another quiche?"

Attorneys and billboards. I've never forgotten that connection Gran made. And Mr. Blackwell was smiling at drivers on billboards from Knoxville to Chattanooga. "If they owe you, you owe it to yourself to CALL US!" I didn't see anything wrong with it. Always wondered where Mr. Brownstone or Mr. Crowley was when the billboard photo was taken, but my guess was they simply couldn't compete with Mr. Blackwell's hair.

The counselor was always friendly to me, but I always felt like a visitor around him, even on the occasions he came to Gran's house to pick up Larry. He never used my name, always calling me "son," which was just plain strange considering I was always in the company of his actual son.

Larry Jr. was my age, but always seemed older to me. Maybe it was because he was always alone when I saw him. (The only other friend I had in Gran's neighborhood — Devon McGee — would play with Larry, but only when I was around.) Like his dad, Larry's hair was jet black, straight as untied shoelaces. And no matter the time of day, Larry had what we now call "bed head." Just enough hair out of place to notice. He combed it; even Larry wanted to look right if we happened to pass Wendy Nickerson. But it just wouldn't stay in place.

Larry was "odd," as Gran put it, but I liked him, mostly because he laughed easily. "Hey Milligan," he'd shout from across the street. "What am I?"

"Dunno, Larry. What are you?"

"That chicken . . . the one that crossed the road!"

That was Larry's material, pretty much all summer. And he'd laugh at these kind of jokes — the ones he told — till his eyes watered.

The one other distinguishing characteristic of Larry Blackwell you should know about — well, physical characteristic — was a large, brown mole he had on the right side of his jaw, just under his ear. The first time we met, three years earlier, I had stared at that mole like I expected it to crawl off his face. ("Wanna pet it, Trey?" he had asked me. Then laughed till his eyes watered.) Gran's housekeeper, Thelma, was convinced that mole was the mark of the devil. In all my years of visiting Gran, it was the only opinion Thelma ever volunteered to me: Larry Blackwell carried the mark of the devil.

* * *

"Why won't you ring the doorbell, young man?" Gran remained mystified at Larry's insistence on knocking on her door — the glass panels, in particular — instead of using a perfectly functioning doorbell.

"Sorry, Ms. Johnson, I forgot." Larry offered the same feeble reply at the beginning of every summer. Gran quit asking after the first visit.

"Wanna go run the neighborhood, Trey?"

From one 13-year-old to another, it was an odd invitation, but it was Larry's way of greeting me, almost every time he walked through Gran's door. He sure wasn't talking about exercising, and the only people we commanded were one another, but to

20

Larry — with me at his side and school out — there was a neighborhood to be "run." So we did.

"I bet you missed Wendy."

I'm not sure if it was taunting, or simply Larry's only known method of cutting to the chase, but once out of Gran's driveway, Larry knew who was on both our minds.

* * *

Gran's neighborhood was a series of winding streets. No "grid" to this part of Cleveland, Tennessee. It was as though developers decided where a house would go based on the curvature of the land (a far cry from the "scraper" mentality of late-20th-century subdivisions). The houses were generally one-story, brick homes. If the backyards were fenced, it was merely chain-link.

There were no lane dividers; traffic was merely homeowners returning from their workday, many of them from Chattanooga. No stoplights or sidewalks, either. Larry and I liked to walk along the nearby streets — Rosemary Lane, Linden Avenue, Cricket Lane, and Gran's street, Westview Drive. We walked because Larry didn't have a bike. The strange part, to me at least, is that Larry didn't *want* a bike.

"When a man walks a neighborhood, people know he belongs," Larry reminded me each summer. "There's time to see the way he steps, where he looks, if he picks his nose in public. What kind of mood he's in. A kid on a bike? He's in too much of a hurry."

The only hill in Gran's neighborhood was Terrace Lane, and the second house from the top of Terrace Lane was the Nickerson home. It was a brown bungalow, with the nicest front porch in Cleveland. Big maple tree in the front yard that shaded the entire house during the summer. At the end of the Nickerson's driveway was a basketball hoop. Not a cheap mobile contraption, but a hoop hung precisely 10 feet high, mounted into the concrete on a pole easily a foot in circumference. The Nickersons even had a free throw line painted 15 feet from the basket. Jerry Nickerson was going to be a senior that fall at Cleveland High School, and was a shoo-in for All-District, if not All-State.

But it was Jerry's sister, Wendy, who had Larry and me wandering up Terrace Lane every June.

Looking back, the best way to describe Wendy Nickerson is the girl who played like a boy, but made a boy — for the first time — think like a man. She and Larry were classmates at Cleveland Junior High, and they were casual friends. But Larry never saw her during the summer without me at his side. Again, Wendy made a 13-year-old boy think differently than he was used to.

"See if she wants to run with us, Trey."

It was my duty — every June — to knock on Wendy's door and essentially request her entry into our summer. My summer, and Larry's. A few years earlier, we'd merely bump into each other at neighborhood barbecues. Ten-year-olds make their own social calendars, but only with grown-ups nearby. But once we moved into our teens — barely, but there — the social calling became our own. With me serving as Larry's calling card.

"She's not going to run with us, Larry. People talk about kids without anything to do, roaming neighborhoods. Like we are right now." And Wendy always had something to do. But I knew how to get her out of the house.

"Well hi, Trey. Nice to see you! Hey Larry." Mrs. Nickerson was a cool mom. She actually seemed excited to see us, and this was every time we came for a visit. What I liked most about Mrs. Nickerson was her straight, dirty-blonde hair. She didn't mess with the perms that became such a rage in the Eighties. She was naturally pretty, just like her daughter.

"Hi, Mrs. Nickerson. We were just wondering if Wendy could play some basketball?" Not only was the Nickerson hoop the only place to play basketball in the neighborhood, but neither Larry nor I had a ball. Asking her to play basketball was a single question with at least three rewards.

"Just a sec, Trey," answered Mrs. Nickerson. "She's back in her room."

3

"So how's the beach, Trey?"

To Wendy, anyone living in California lived on (or near) "the beach." My canvas Nike sneakers were exotic to Wendy, just like the Rags I called pants (it was actually a name brand). Conversations with Wendy started with the dribble of a basketball as the back-beat. Long before we knew the expression "ice-breaker," basketball served as our entree to the world of the only girl Larry and I had the courage to make our friend.

"Not as humid as it is here," I offered, before clanking my first shot off Wendy's basket. (I played for an undefeated 7th-grade team back home, but was a scrub off the bench. Scored exactly 17 points in 12 games.) "You really need to get your parents to take you to the Carolina coast. There are beaches closer than California, Wendy."

"But *the* beach, Trey, will always be California. That's where stars get their suntans, you know. Not that your suntan matches Sly's."

Wendy loved Sylvester Stallone. Which pretty much disqualified Larry and me from the category of possibilities for this jump-shooting starlet in our midst. Larry did have the black hair though.

"Why's the beach so great?" asked Larry. "We go to the muni pool here in town and we have everything you find at the beach except sand and crabs."

"Sounds just like someone who's never been to the beach," snorted Wendy after draining a shot from her painted foul line. "That's okay, Larry. I'll tell you all about it when Trey finally takes me."

The thought of taking Wendy anywhere in the world was inspiring, even if I was merely the ticket to getting her within shouting distance of Rocky Balboa. Like her mom, Wendy wore her dirty blonde hair — there was nothing dirty about it — straight, beyond the shoulders, often in a ponytail when summer arrived. She wore sleeveless tops, bright colors, but nothing we came to see as "feminine." No butterflies, no flowers, no horses even.

The only symbols I remember seeing on Wendy Nickerson were those of her Atlanta Braves, whether it was a screaming, mohawked Native American, the cursive capital 'A' the team wore on its hats, or merely a tomahawk. Wendy played basketball, but she loved baseball, particularly her Braves. Which, of course, made me love her, my loyalties to the Cardinals be damned.

Basketball gets boring with odd numbers, and

Larry couldn't dribble to begin with. Not that he tried. He was here for Wendy's company.

"Wanna run the neighborhood?" That expression again.

"Where are you going?" asked Wendy. "Not the Hanky-Panky. I don't have any money."

The Hanky-Panky was the convenience store, a couple of miles and several blocks away. I had bought baseball cards by the dozen at the Hanky-Panky, one summer after the next. But I was *not* to walk there.

"Let's go down to Crawdad Creek," said Larry. "I've got smokes."

Behind Gran's house, down a steep, wooded hill, was what we called Crawdad Creek. Perfect name, considering the shallow stream's chief inhabitants. It was really the only place to get away in this section of Cleveland. Gran's neighborhood had too many walkers, strollers, even bikers. Streets meandered in such a way that nosy neighbors were around every turn. But down at Crawdad Creek — whether it was to catch crawdads or for more nefarious reasons — kids could grow up. At least in our minds.

"I'm not smoking with you, Larry." Wendy saw her older brother smoke, didn't like the smell, and wasn't prepared to cultivate a taste for cigarettes. "It doesn't make you cool, you know. It makes you stink. And your teeth turn yellow."

"You don't have to smoke, Nickerson," snorted Larry. "I know Trey won't. But a man's gotta have his fix."

"Running" the neighborhood. And a "man" getting his "fix." The world Larry broadcast from his brain and mouth was a few moonshots away from the world in which he actually lived. But he was entertaining. And a partner for visits to Wendy's driveway.

"Hey Trey, come over Sunday for the Braves game," said Wendy. "They're playing the Reds." The best thing about this trio was baseball, because it was the one bond shared entirely — and only — by Wendy and me. An invitation to watch a Braves game was the closest I'd ever come to a date with Wendy. And on those three-hour visits, I couldn't imagine wanting to be anywhere else on the planet, including an actual ballpark.

"Sure. Sounds good. But you know," I reminded her as she scooped up her ball and headed inside, "the Braves can't play with St. Louis."

"I'll see you Sunday, Trey," she smiled back. "Take it easy, Larry."

* * *

"She's growing a pair, Trey. Won't be long."

For three years now, Wendy had been "growing

28

a pair" according to Larry. I never knew if Larry saw the charms in Wendy I knew were there, or if it was merely the anticipation of her becoming a woman — someday, and not only in his world — that attracted him to her. What I did know is that the things I saw in Wendy Nickerson (and the things I remember today) had nothing to do with a "pair" she was growing.

"You know, Larry, she'll be on her front porch someday, wearing a bikini. Sunglasses on, probably with that basketball she was just shooting. You'll wander up, and you won't know what to do. You won't know what to say, how to stand, whether to sit down or turn around to run home. You'll just be staring . . . at her pair."

Larry laughed. Hard and loudly. Eyes squinted almost shut. Because he got the joke, and knew it was one-hundred percent true.

4

I had three friends, really, who shaped my summers in Cleveland. There was Larry, who made the days pass quicker. There was Wendy, who filled my thoughts during quiet time. But it was Devon McGee who changed my life that last summer at Gran's. Like most people who impact your life outside your family, Devon never intended to change mine. And I certainly never saw it coming.

The McGees were the only black family in Gran's neighborhood. They were also one of the few families with two working adults. Mr. and Mrs. McGee ran a travel agency in Chattanooga: Cruises and Coasts. It was just the two of them, which seemed like cheating, somehow, to me. A married couple wakes up together. They come home, have dinner, and go to bed together. But spend the day together? Earn a living together? If it was cheating, I admired the McGees nonetheless. And I knew it had to be true love for a husband and wife to work together. Easy enough to drive a person away when they're *not* your business partner.

It says much about Devon — six months older than me — that his parents let him stay home by himself that summer. Thirteen years old, still in junior high, and they left him home. The McGees lived next door to a retired couple — the Weatherbys — and like everyone who met Devon, they adored him. Had there been an emergency, Devon's instructions were to go straight to the Weatherbys and stay with them until his parents got home. But there weren't any emergencies, at least not until the 4th of July weekend, and the McGees were home together then.

Devon was tiny. Not small. Tiny. I was tall for my age, a shade under 5'10" (with no more vertical growth in my future). The top of Devon's head — and he styled himself a mini-Afro, in part to gain height — didn't reach my armpits. He was a little guy. He liked basketball enough, though resented the assumption on the part of strangers. ("When someone sees my blackness and assumes I play basketball," he wondered, "do they not see my height, too?'") Whether or not he distanced himself from hoops because of his own self-awareness about size, Devon's true love was his bike. He rode it everywhere.

Devon's bike was orange. There's no other way to put it: the bike was ugly. But it was always shiny, tires always full, chain tight. Devon even had the kickstand just the right feel: not too tight to kick down, not so loose it would fall on its own. He loved that bike and resented another assumption, that the bike was a reflection of his devotion to the University of Tennessee Volunteers. The only orange Devon cared about was the layer of paint on his bike.

Size was one thing, but health another, and Devon was a diabetic. Every day, he gave himself a shot of insulin. Just pinched an inch or two of his stomach and stuck a needle in. It was the kind of routine self-maintenance that horrified me to consider and would horrify most kids to practice, but Devon took care of himself as he'd been taught. Remember, the McGee house was his on summer days. He was that responsible. Diabetes didn't hinder him, at least not in the eyes of Wendy, Larry, or me. Devon smiled more than the rest of us, probably combined. And always on that bike, whether he was actually going somewhere — he lived on the other side of Crawdad Creek, behind Gran's house — or riding in circles. If that was a sick boy amongst us, then I needed to check myself into a hospital.

* * *

"What are you doing with that pansy, Trey?"

If Devon and Larry every greeted each other without an insult, I didn't hear it.

"Isn't pansy a big word for such a small guy?" retorted Larry. Only Larry would define "pansy" as

32

being a big word.

"What're you guys doing?" asked Devon, looking at me as he actually stopped peddling and dropped a foot to the asphalt.

"I'm heading back to Gran's. Supper time."

"You happen to be coming back from Wendy's?"

"Yeah, Trey just finished with her in the Nickersons' garage." Classy, that Larry.

"She kick your asses again at hoop?"

"We just shot around a little," I said. "Not enough time for a game."

"Let's go down to the creek tomorrow," suggested Larry. "I've got smokes. And *Playboy*." I'd like to think Devon and I were moral standards beyond Larry Blackwell's reach, but we were best friends whenever his dad got a new issue of *Playboy*.

"Just call me," shouted Devon as he wheeled away. The sun was near setting. His supper would be ready soon, too.

5

The sound of the lawn mower at 8:00 Saturday morning was as regular during my summers in Cleveland as a thunder shower, just more predictable. It meant Flossie was mowing her yard.

Flossie Hillgarten was Gran's next-door neighbor, and best friend within shouting distance. And Flossie did her share of shouting, in part because so many of her conversations — with Gran and others — were conducted over the steady roar of her lawn mower.

Flossie was a widow, as Gran described her to anyone who asked. But the only black I ever saw her wear was her bra. You see, Flossie mowed her yard — every Saturday morning, like *The Bugs Bunny and Road Runner Show* — in a pair of short-shorts and a bra. Always black.

"Mawnin', Trey! I thought I saw you strollin' the other day. Summa must be heah."

I couldn't help it, and Gran never stopped me. Being greeted by a woman wearing nothing but a bra on Saturday morning was more than I could pass up. Oh, I'd act like I was grabbing a seat on Gran's patio to read a comic book, as though it was the only spot on Gran's property where Spider-Man and I could fully commiserate. But that lawn mower was calling me.

"Morning, Flossie. Good to see you."

Flossie was only a few years younger than Gran, but not for lack of effort. You don't see the kind of blonde hair Flossie had on a woman older than 20. And lipstick applied that thick was usually for Saturday night, on stage in front of an audience, not Saturday morning, behind a lawn mower, in front of adolescent boys. On just the other side of Gran's chain-link fence — it represented the leftfield line of my backyard ballpark — was adulthood. To this day, Flossie never so much as shook my hand. But our relationship is one that, with the help of girls like Wendy Nickerson, turned me into a man.

"You know who you need to visit, Trey?" Flossie would open a line of conversation as she turned the mower alongside the shared fence between her house and Gran's. "Arline Varden. She asks about you every winter, you know."

With my eyes being pulled between the web-slinger and the already-sweating cleavage that seemed to steer Flossie along her gardening mission, I nodded toward Flossie, hearing the pitch I knew was coming. "Arline comes over and walks Rascal when I'm in Florida. She's seen your picture on my fridge. And she's your age, Trey!"

It was as if Flossie didn't see me the countless hours I was in that yard — didn't have to be Saturday — hurling a ball against Gran's patio deck, training for my first big-league contract. To Flossie, I was a young man, and young men needed young women. The nearest young woman to Flossie — someone she knew only through a beauty-parlor connection — was Arline Varden. Which made Arline and me a perfect match.

* * *

Arline lived in a trailer park — I always found that cool — behind Gran's house, on the other side of Crawdad Creek. She was a year younger than Larry, Devon, and me, which might as well have placed her in kindergarten according to Larry. ("If they're not sprouting, I ain't shouting," Larry would announce when clarifying his taste in women. Dude was crass.)

The thing about Arline, though, is that she wasn't shy. Not around boys, not around older boys. She had an older sister in high school — Michelle — and you got the feeling Arline had seen some "action" guys like Larry only bragged about. Arline's mom didn't work, and her dad was a builder, a "contractor" as they call them now. Income was sporadic for the Vardens — thus the trailer park — but I can't recall seeing Arline in a bad mood. She had long brown hair, and eyes the color of polished furniture . . . dark polished furniture. Arline's laugh was her own, too. It was rough, a smoker's laugh you'd call it, except from lungs clean of cigarettes and the like. She had a raspy laugh, is all. I liked it.

Arline had one remarkable skill: "dialin'." The local radio station — WCLE — played rock-and-roll; I learned to like Billy Joel, Fleetwood Mac, and Blondie by listening to WCLE. Every weeknight, WCLE would give away a free album to a certain caller.

"Listen up, Cleveland," deejay Bobbie Backwoods would announce. "It's time to dial! The 12th caller will have themselves a copy of the latest from Stevie Nicks."

This was a simple time in telecommunications. Most families had as many rotary phones as they did push-button. But the Vardens had a push-button, and it may as well have been a musical instrument in Arline's hands. She could dial the studio number — 555-9253 — faster than I could recite the number. And the girl could time her call with an accuracy beyond any adult's grasp, let alone a child's. Starting late in her 5th-grade year at Cleveland Elementary, Arline had been winning records. That first summer, she had 20 albums before August, when WCLE actually sent her a "policy letter," explaining that in the interest of their listening audience, she needed to stop dialing, and allow some other winners.

Didn't stop Arline. She simply found friends to take the receiver from her after she dialed. Fresh voice, new address. And if Arline didn't like the album being offered, she simply gave it to her newly enlisted partner in crime. (It's how I ended up with a Jackson Browne LP I never listened to.) It was the thrill of "dialin'" that brought Arline to the phone each night. She was good at it. She knew it. And she flaunted it.

Which is what brought me to her house on a Thursday night in late June.

6

"Trey, it's Arline on the phone."

Gran was never surprised when Arline called out of the blue. Like I said, she wasn't shy. And she knew where to find me when summer arrived.

"Hey Arline. What's up?"

"I'm dialin' tonight, Trey. Will you come over? You can be on the radio." It was the same pitch, every time. As though being heard to say, "Wow, thanks Bobbie!," on airwaves throughout greater Cleveland, Tennessee, would have me on my way to Hollywood.

Walking down the hill behind Gran's house, through the trees and across Crawdad Creek — a fat tree trunk bridged the water at a narrow section about 100 yards south of Gran's house — I enjoyed the approach to Arline's trailer park. It wasn't so much as a statement on socio-economic condition as it was a different world from the one I knew, one where picnic tables accompanied driveways, "above-ground-pools" sat behind the well-to-do trailers, and the fanciest homes included an awning that made a shady patch of dust the equivalent of a front porch. The Vardens had an awning. It was bright green.

"Hurry up, Trey! It's almost 7:30!!"

Half-past seven was "dialin'" time at WCLE. The only missing variable was which caller would be tonight's winner. Bobbie Backwoods usually kept it under 10 — "Caller number eight is a winna!" — but he'd throw out a "13th caller" or "21st caller" when he felt impetuous. This wasn't one of those nights.

"Hi, Mrs. Varden. Arline's dialing, I hear." Mrs. Varden would have been beautiful — gorgeous, really — about 40 pounds ago. Her hair was still chestnut brown. And she loved wearing tank tops. (Again, 40 pounds ago, she would have made heads turn.) But however much weight she'd gained since her cheerleading days at Cleveland High, Theresa Varden still had a smile like sunshine. (Remember how a smile never ages? Somehow, the same rule applies with weight gain.)

"Hey there, Trey. You hustle back to the den and be ready to get yourself a new record. I'm makin' milkshakes for you kids."

What Mrs. Varden called her "den" was really the only room in the trailer. She and Mr. Varden shared a bedroom that would be better described as a compartment and, on the other side of a bathroom, Arline managed to fit a cot and all her stuffed animals into . . . a closet. (As for the bathroom, it was a shower the size of a phone booth, a toilet, and a sink. I never tried it, but I think you could have used all three without taking a single step.) I hardly ever saw all four Vardens at home at the same time. In a place so small, how could four people gather comfortably, even for a TV dinner? Didn't help Michelle's reputation that she was never at home. Never occurred to me that it didn't help Arline's either.

It may have been small, but Arline's "den" was fun. A couch filled it from one end (the refrigerator) to the other (her parents' bedroom). Mr. Varden had installed a TV shelf above the window opposite the couch, with a card table below for snacks, meals, and Mrs. Varden's milkshakes. Also resting on that table was the Vardens' only phone . . . a weapon in Arline's hands.

"It's Thursday niiiiiiiight, Cleveland! It's time for some free rock-and-roll. I said *FREE* rock-and-roll! You've heard the new Hall & Oates hit. Gimme a call and you'll have a copy of their new album. Caller number nine is a winna!"

All you could do at this point was watch Arline. More specifically, watch Arline's fingers. Already off its base, the black phone was an instrument — weapon, if you prefer — that Arline played like it was an extension of her arm. 555-9253. There might be a busy signal, and she'd use her non-dialing hand (her left) to press the base's switch just low enough to disconnect . . . and dial again. It wasn't for another year that I noticed the most captivating part of Arline's dialing skill: she never blinked. No air traffic controller has been born with more focus than Arline Varden on "dialin' night."

"HERE, TREY! Take it-take it-take it!!"

She'd won again.

"We've got a winna, Cleveland! Caller number nine, you are on the line at WCLE with B-B-Bobbie Backwoods. What do you call yourself?"

"Uh, hey Bobbie. I'm David Green." (I always used the name of St. Louis Cardinal players. Green was a backup outfielder. Bobbie Backwoods didn't know squat about sports.)

"Well, David, you are the new owner of *H2O*, the latest hit from America's rock-and-roll dynamic duo, Hall & Oates!!"

"Cool . . . thanks Bobbie!"

"Hang on the line, David, and we'll have this RCA hit on its way before sunup tomorrow. For the rest of you Cleveland rockers, enjoy 'Maneater.'"

After giving Bobbie's assistant Flossie's address, the deal was done. (The entire neighborhood knew of Arline's gift and was perfectly willing to help launder her winnings. Made older folks like Flossie feel like they were contributing to something illicit, and I guess they were.)

"I KNEW I'd win tonight, Trey. We won last summer the first time you spoke for me." (Arline had won all three times I "spoke for her" last summer. I felt less like a good-luck charm and more like a necessary conspirator.)

"Chocolate peppermint, kids. Enjoy. And I want to hear that record the day it arrives, Arline."

Mrs. Varden was the real winner in her family's expanding musical library. If the tunes inspired her to blend pieces of peppermint into her chocolate shakes, I was going to help in this endeavor as long as Arline would have me.

"Braves are on. Playing the Phillies tonight, I think."

Arline knew how to keep me interested. She was no Wendy when it came to the Braves — or baseball in general — but she knew how to socialize, even at twelve.

"I'd take Dale Murphy over Mike Schmidt any day."

"Have you heard of George Hendrick?" I tried to educate Arline — well, anyone really — about my Cardinals. But it didn't quite take.

"I haven't heard of George Hendrix," Arline retorted. "Which means he's not as good as Dale Murphy . . . or Mike Schmidt. Have you seen Wendy yet?"

Arline could turn a conversation on its ear. And despite being a year older, I always seemed to let her steer.

"Yeah," I told her. "Larry and I went to shoot hoops at her place earlier this week." Never would I hint that I went to Wendy's house to, you know, see Wendy.

"Do you like her, Trey?"

"Sure, as a friend," I lied. "She's cool. Even though she likes the Braves." A baseball insult aimed in two directions at the same time.

"Tell me this, Trey, Mr. John Hendrix. If Wendy didn't have a basketball net or a baseball glove, would you go to see her? Would you take Larrrrrrry to see her?!"

Unfair question. Who the hell was Arline to assume motive, much less assume attraction on my part?

"I'd go see her, I guess. Aren't that many kids in the neighborhood, you know."

And this hurt Arline. I could tell because she went at least five minutes — minutes that changed my life — without taking another sip of that chocolate/peppermint milkshake.

"I'm in the neighborhood, Trey. I've always been here, in the neighborhood. But the only time you ever come to my house is when I ask you over on dialin' night. If there aren't enough kids in the neighborhood, why don't you come to my house? I'm not kid enough?"

This was getting heavier than any chat Arline and I had ever had. Because she was right on. I always considered Arline a younger girl. She was closer to Libby in my eyes than she was to competition for Wendy Nickerson. I would have been less surprised to see Arline Varden playing with my 8-year-old sister than I would have seeing her walk the same clouds Wendy did in my mind. She was a younger girl; simple as that.

"I've come to see you, Arline." Another lie. "You're not always here, and I don't always knock. Sometimes Larry and I walk to Hanky Panky, right down the road." Hanky Panky was the stop-and-shop where I got my baseball cards. And I was not to walk there on my own . . . or with Larry. More on that later.

"Why don't you ever come over to Gran's house?" And this was an unfair question from me, so we're even. No way does Arline knock on a boy's house uninvited. She may be 12 years old, but this is the South.

"Okay, I owe you a visit," she said. "I'll call first, and you better not say don't come."

Then she kissed me. Arline Varden kissed me. The Phillies were batting, in the top of the third.

* * *

It's strange, but not surprising, really. The "life-changing" events we experience are hardly ever anticipated, and they're usually as brief as a first kiss . . . on the right cheek. But part of the life-changing nature of such events is the heightened sensory condition that we can reflect upon the rest of our lives.

I remember the taste of Mrs. Varden's chocolate peppermint milkshake in my mouth from the moment Arline leaned over and changed my childhood forever. I remember staring in silence at her TV, watching the Phillies go down in order. (Mike Schmidt flew out to left, Bo Diaz struck out, and Garry Maddox grounded to short.)

I also remember not hearing a thing, not the voices of Skip Carray and Ernie Johnson on the broadcast, not Mrs. Varden (outside, drinking tea and reading *Cosmopolitan*), and most of all, nothing from Arline. We sat there. In complete silence, as if nothing had happened . . . and it had changed the world.

A milkshake is perfect for such silences. Awkward or otherwise, a shake is to be enjoyed slowly, with steady pulls on the straw. It's understood that savoring and swallowing a milkshake takes time, so obligatory chatter is swept aside like yesterday's worries. Those milkshakes probably saved my friendship with Arline that night. Because if I didn't have it to help me absorb the moment, to let Arline's tender gesture find its way from my cheek to my heart, I certainly would have embarrassed myself with whatever I came up with to say. And I wouldn't have survived the lifelong trauma of being reminded of my clumsy tongue. Or again, my friendship with Arline wouldn't have survived such trauma.

But the shakes did their thing. The Braves came back up in the bottom of the third and Bob Horner hit a home run to give Atlanta the lead. Horner was the other Brave (besides Dale Murphy) Arline knew, so she was part of the game again.

"You know, Trey. I'd even take Bob Horner over George Hendrix."

"It's Hendrick, Arline. H-E-N-D-R-I-C-K. With a C-K. No X."

We watched the rest of that game, the only one I remember seeing the final out in the Varden trailer. Arline and I talked about everything except what was actually on our mind. I'd imagined for three summers what it would be like to kiss Wendy Nickerson on the cheek. And not be slapped for it. I'd never imagined what it would be like to be kissed on the cheek by Wendy Nickerson. And I'd never considered how good it would feel to be kissed on the cheek by Arline Varden. I was many moons, yet, from becoming a man. But I sure wasn't a boy any more.

7

Mattie Clay Caldwell was Gran's older sister. Fourteen years older. She was 78 the last summer I saw her, suffering arthritis to the point her hands were claws, her legs all but useless. She was petrified of dogs, never bought me a toy . . . and has come to embody class and dignity in ways I couldn't quite envision when I was 13. She was known as "Auntie" by those of us who loved her.

Auntie lived her last two years in the Springview Senior Center, a place not nearly as comforting as its name. High on a hill above Highway 64 that brought traffic to and from Chattanooga, Springview — to this day — makes me scared of getting old. As clean as a model home on Saturday morning, Springview had its own smell that somehow twisted the sensory impression of its hallways into one of dread, even fear if you were there at the wrong time of day. The smell was sweet, but a warm, overdone — spoiled — sweet. Like carrots gone bad.

The residents of Springview strolled its halls freely. There was no Nurse Ratched, no bars behind windows, no doors missing their handle. Some were in wheelchairs, many had walkers, a lucky few strong enough to stroll one wing of the center before taking in the latest episode of *Dallas* or *Dynasty* in the community room.

Auntie didn't stroll the halls of Springview. And she sure didn't stare at a television or card table in the community room. Best I could tell, she rested in her bed and waited for the next visit from her family. All the while in pain, her joints screaming that life had given her all she could expect . . . why was she sticking around?

Gran cared for Auntie out of familial duty. She was the closest of Auntie's four living siblings, geographically and emotionally. The 14-year age difference gave Auntie a supervisory position, though, ironic as she lay handicapped in a bed under what amounted to 24-hour surveillance. We never went as many as four days without visiting Auntie, Libby armed with coloring books, me with my baseball cards. Gran needed to check in and lift Auntie's spirits, and also to show off the children she could claim as *her* grandchildren. (We were Auntie's grandchildren, too, as she never had kids of her own. Gran knew this, and there was actually some rivalry that flavored their relationship near the end of Auntie's life.)

"How are those beautiful children?"

Auntie's smile — remember, they never age — was indomitable. I wasn't old enough to fully understand aging, but I sure as hell could recognize a body in pain. How was Auntie smiling every time we entered her room?

"Did you even bring in your newspaper? What's it doing in the hall, on the bench?"

Gran entered Auntie's room with a critical eye. This was important, because details matter when a loved one is ailing. But it also made Gran hyper-critical when it came to the way Auntie's room was presented, something she had very little control over. Least of all, whether or not an attendant actually brought her newspaper to her bedside stand.

"I had CNN on all morning, Cooper. There's nothing the *Cleveland Daily Press* can tell me that Ted Turner hasn't already."

"I colored you a picture, Auntie. It's of you, me, and Princess Leia." Libby had enjoyed *The Empire Strikes Back* enough to buy the bubble-gum cards. I suppose if Darth Vader could be Luke Skywalker's father, our crippled great-aunt could stroll in a meadow with Princess Leia.

"Libby, this should hang in a museum!"

It's an ironic part of the human condition that we can't see the face of a person we hug. A physical reality, sure, but think about it: hugs are faceless.

Every time I hugged Auntie, I did so gently. I already outweighed her. I knew how tender her body was, how the stabs of pain came without warning, and from slight movement, let alone the squeeze of an overdue hug. And every time I hugged Auntie, I'm sure her body grimaced. But it was always a smile that greeted me again when we unlocked our arms. Auntie loved life . . . but not as much as she loved Libby and me.

"Tell me what you're reading today, Trey."

The truth was, I hadn't read anything besides *Sports Illustrated* and Spider-Man comics since school let out three weeks ago.

"Bless the Beasts and Children," I lied. At least I'd read it in Ms. Morgan's English class that spring.

"That's a good one, Trey. You'll be a wise man if you keep reading; you're already a wise boy."

Gran placed a green-bean casserole on the single — tiny — table in Auntie's room. Her last name was written on the foil that covered the dish, as it would be swept away to the kitchen the next time one of Springview's smiling, over-worked nurses checked in on Auntie. (Just how much green-bean casserole Auntie would later enjoy depended on how appetizing Gran's meal appeared to nurse staff. Gran knew this, and considered it a down payment for some extra TLC for her sister.) Gran never mentioned the food she dropped off and, strangely, Auntie never thanked her. Sisters just have an understanding, I supposed. Gran and Auntie understood each other well.

"Have you been outside this week?" asked Gran. Springview had a decent courtyard, a pair of fountains flanking a garden with sunflowers, daisies, and the like.

"Hilda took me for a walk just this morning," replied Auntie. (Hilda was her favorite nurse, a black woman who tipped the scales at 200 pounds on her lightest day. She adored Auntie, though. I later learned that Hilda's mom had suffered arthritis. Like Gran and Auntie, Hilda and Auntie understood each other well.) "You know I don't like the humidity, but the sunshine helps my spirits. Does sunshine help your spirits, Libby?"

My sister was already coloring a new scene, one she would rush to finish in the 30 or 40 minutes we'd be with Auntie. "I like it when there are rainbows!" Not sure if Libby knew what her spirits were, but they were always in decent shape, rain, shine, or rainbows.

"How are your parents, Trey?"

This was a loaded question, coming from Auntie. If there was one single person most responsible for my parents' higher academic

pursuits, it wasn't any of my grandparents. Not even
Gran. It was Auntie. When tuition money was short,
Auntie was always there. ("You know, I have $5,000
that I just don't plan on using," she'd tell my dad.
"See what you and Melinda might be able to get for
your family.") Neither side of my family was
destitute by any means, but we were hardly flush
with cash, either. If there was a matriarch — a
godmother? — it was this tiny, hobbled, delicate
woman losing a battle with arthritis, all the while
winning a war against any force that might get in the
way of her family's growth. What I didn't know then
was that it was as much business for Auntie as
affection. And she knew how to run a business.

* * *

Auntie and her late husband, Ed — he was
known as "Uncle" by my mom's generation — had
owned and run a department store in Etowah,
Tennessee. Caldwell's was unique to Etowah, a town
with as many stoplights and gas stations as it had
department stores. When Mom later told me Etowah
had 5,000 residents, I would have guessed no more
than 500. But it had shoppers with taste in clothes,
and Auntie provided for that market.

She had hair the precise color of her antique
furniture, at least that's the way I remember it now.
(Gran's color of choice was blonde, a shiny yellow

that may not have made her look younger, but sure made her appear warm . . . sunshine to her grandchildren.) The times when she took Libby and me out — before she got too sick, and before Libby and I could really appreciate the outings — Auntie always wore a dress, with high heels. I'd have a baseball cap pulled down near the bridge of my nose and Libby would be prancing around in shorts and one of her "picture shirts" (she loved the Smurfs). But Auntie was the picture of style in public. Her purse, it should be noted, always matched her shoes.

While Gran and Granddaddy provided toys, comic books, and baseball cards, Auntie took it upon herself to make sure we dressed the part of Southern aristocrats. Just like the drives and lessons she'd teach — "A gentleman allows a lady to enter a car first, Trey." — the clothes came too early for Libby and me to appreciate. But when school began each fall, and our clothes were top of the line (I had boots with a zipper!), our teachers appreciated the role Mattie Clay Caldwell played in our lives. Mom and Dad sure did.

* * *

"They're fine, Auntie," I said. How did I know if my parents were well, here three weeks into my third Southern summer getaway? Didn't matter. All was well in Gran's world, even at the Springview Senior

Center.

"Wanna go outside, Auntie? We'll push you!"

Libby loved to stroll in the courtyard, but didn't quite understand how long it took Auntie to summon the strength to transfer from her bed to her wheelchair. Even if she couldn't take such a stroll, she fed on my sister's enthusiasm.

"Why, Libby, I'd love to go outside with you. But you know what, I know your grandmother has a special dinner planned tonight, and I don't want to keep you tied up here too late." Auntie could spin with the best of them. Gently, but she could spin a tale. I've come to realize that as much as she loved seeing Libby and me — and Gran, of course — the visits were tiring. Take your wrist and twist it till it won't twist any more. Hold it there for 10 minutes . . . and smile. That was Auntie's challenge near the end. Fight her body's invader 24 hours a day . . . but make sure to smile for me and Libby. To this day, I've yet to meet a stronger person.

"I know Larry King's on tonight," Gran said as she leaned over to kiss Auntie's forehead. "Is Hilda watching with you? Or Martha?" Martha was Auntie's next-door neighbor.

"I'll watch him if I'm up, Cooper." Auntie would commit to nothing. "Martha hasn't been by in days." She preferred Hilda's company, but would never tell a fellow resident.

"We'll be back to see you day after tomorrow," said Gran. "Make sure you get your newspaper. Keeps your mind sharp in ways CNN can't."

Libby hugged Auntie's right shoulder, as much as she could grab. And Auntie winced. I leaned over and kissed her cheek. I knew a gentle stroke of her hand was as good as a hug these days.

"I love you, children. And I'm so proud of you!"

Funny how a 13-year-old boy searches for love among his peers, that mysterious, vexing opposite sex that seems to make no sense. And all the while, true love surrounds him in the presence of a woman made less mysterious, somehow, by the passage of time.

8

It's the only time I ever cried at Gran's house. Well, the only time I ever cried out of fear. Had nothing to do with dark rooms, bullies, or even Wendy Nickerson. Didn't involve pain or illness, not in the least.

It was the time Gran caught me lying. The time I *knew* she caught me lying.

Larry and I were fairly free to roam the neighborhood . . . but there were boundaries. Well-defined boundaries. On Gran's side of Crawdad Creek, there were six blocks, each with between seven and ten houses. (Wendy's was three blocks and two houses from Gran's.) If we asked permission, we could cross the Creek to visit Arline in the trailer park.

But that was it. Further into Cleveland — "the city" in Gran's eyes — and we'd be runaways. Gran's car was for visits to "the city." Our feet were to stay on the sidewalks and streets on Gran's side of Crawdad Creek.

The Hanky-Panky was, alas, beyond Crawdad Creek, beyond Arline's trailer park. Eleven blocks — including three turns through a neighborhood that surrounded Cleveland Junior High — beyond Arline's trailer park. I knew each of these 11 blocks because Larry had walked them with me every summer I'd visited from California. He taught me this route like a postal carrier would in passing his torch to a new generation. We were wandering explorers in Larry's eyes, and the Hanky-Panky was our oasis.

Larry's vices were beef jerky and girly magazines, and both were stocked in quantity at the Hanky-Panky. Ms. Linda ran the place — at least during the daylight hours when Larry and I would visit — and she never took her nose out of the latest tabloid long enough to notice Larry snag a copy of *Playboy* or *Penthouse* on our way back to the candy aisle. (It was actually at the end of the candy aisle where we'd stick our noses in our own periodical, back where Ms. Linda stocked the Krispy Kreme donuts and Little Debbie snack cakes. Out of view.)

"I'd take care of her, no doubt," Larry would start. Neither of us had any idea what "taking care of" a woman meant. But it sounded good — dirty *and* good, somehow — and I'd nod my head in agreement. If Larry could take care of Miss June, you're darn right I could.

"She's an eight-and-a-half," Trey. "Hair's too curly." About the only honest taste Larry had in the fairer sex was his devotion to straight hair. He'd fallen in love with Peggy Lipton watching reruns of *The Mod Squad*. And a woman's hair had to be straight — however little clothing she was wearing — to merit top rank in Larry's fantasy scheme of womanhood.

"But you know what? She reminds me of Wendy. No?"

"You're full of it, Larry. The only thing that chick and Wendy have in common are two eyes and two ears."

"Ah, ah, ah . . . Trey, c'mon. They share two more things. You know it!"

Larry's crush on Wendy Nickerson was as shallow as Crawdad Creek. Which made his allusions to her — centered on sex, always on sex — all the more irritable to me. I could love Wendy, I honestly believed. And I didn't need to be picturing her braces in the smile on Miss June.

"I'm getting baseball cards, man. When you're finished drooling, get your jerky and let's go. I don't want Gran calling your house."

Depending on how much allowance I'd saved — Gran gave me five dollars, every Saturday; Libby, too — I'd get three to five packs of baseball cards, at fifty cents a pack. Ms. Linda would have a box of Topps near the checkout counter, on what would now be called a "clearance island." But it was right where I needed it to be.

My method was simple. Never take the top pack. And never dig to the bottom of the box (too greedy). With 15 cards per pack, the likelihood of getting at least one Cardinal was fairly good with at least three packs. (This was a time when there were 26 teams in the big leagues, and Topps printed cards of entire teams, including the third-string catchers.)

I'd open my first pack on the sidewalk outside the Hanky-Panky, on a bench Ms. Linda kept there, it seemed, just for this occasion. Then I'd take the rest home to Gran's before opening them. Like with so many things in life — including Larry's lengthy preoccupation inside while I opened my first pack — it was the anticipation of baseball-card collecting that made it joyous. Fulfillment came regularly and often — when Ozzie Smith or Keith Hernandez jumped into my palm — but that anticipation of Ozzie *maybe*, no *probably* being in *this precise pack* . . . yep, joyous. Unwrapping a pack of baseball cards was every bit as exciting as the thought of unwrapping Miss June. Larry never figured that out.

"Here ya go." I'd never call Larry generous, but he always offered me a stick of beef jerky for the walk home. It was cheap — Red Injun was the unfortunate brand — and it took 30 minutes to chew through a single stick. Just long enough for the walk back to Gran's.

* * *

"We're out of milk."

Four words you never heard Gran say. Her kitchen was stocked with every food group . . . and reserves for every food group. I should have known with those four words — "We're out of milk." — that this would be a day I'd never forget.

"Fetch Libby and let's go to the Hanky-Panky. I know you won't mind a pack of baseball cards."

Gran didn't know I'd been to the Hanky-Panky the day before, with Larry. And she wasn't going to find out. In my simple mind, she wasn't going to find out.

"Can I get a blow-pop?" Libby's Hanky-Panky treasures weren't as refined as mine, but she had her own delights. And a lollipop with gum in the middle made the inconvenience of loading into the car rather mild.

I always rode shotgun in Gran's Buick sedan, Libby in the backseat with the stuffed animals and dolls she chose to leave there 24 hours a day. The drives we took with Gran were passages of a sort. I felt older, and she felt younger. (Somehow we met in the middle by listening to Slim Whitman on her 8-track player.)

"Oh, law . . . I missed the turn." Gran's version of an expletive was "oh, law." Never figured out if it was an abbreviated "lord," or a reference to, you know, the law, police.

Gran took Cumberland Avenue — Cleveland's central thoroughfare — anywhere she went, whether it was a trip to Etowah to check on Auntie's house or merely a five-minute drive to the Hanky-Panky. She could access and navigate that road blind-folded.

But I knew another route.

"Turn there, Gran, on the left." I didn't know the name of the street, or I didn't pay attention to it. But it happened to be merely a block away from Larry's house. I'd crossed it hundreds of times.

"Turn here, you say?," asked Gran.

"Yeah, it's easy."

"Hmmmmmmm . . . alright, then. Let's see where Chippawah Road takes us."

Two blocks down Chippawah — at my instruction — Gran took a right. We passed the back side of Arline's trailer park before taking another right.

"Just take a left at the stop sign, and it's about a block."

Gran slowed at the neighborhood's only four-way stop. And she paused longer than it seemed she had to, which made me wonder. Turns out, she was wondering, too.

"So the Hanky-Panky is just a block down yonder?" We were turning onto Dylan Avenue, which intersected Cumberland Avenue . . . but on the other side of Hanky-Panky.

"Yep." I had changed in the eyes of my grandmother with that simple, one-syllable affirmation. And I still had no idea.

Gran turned into the gravel lot in front of Hanky-Panky, parked the car and turned off the ignition. "You two wait here. I won't be two minutes."

"Can I get some baseball cards?"

"Wait here, Trey. And watch your sister."

Something was wrong. This wasn't a family trip to Hanky-Panky anymore.

When Gran returned, she handed a blow-pop to Libby. Her favorite flavor, grape. Nary a pack of baseball cards.

We drove back to Gran's house in silence . . . and along Cumberland Avenue.

The rest of the day seemed normal. I played baseball in the backyard. No visit from Larry or Devon. Watched *Alice* with Libby. Sorted my Cardinals team set as if it needed sorting. And enjoyed Gran's macaroni and cheese, made lovingly with the milk we'd bought at Hanky-Panky.

After dinner, as I was munching on a Brown Cow ice cream bar, Gran came into the den and sat down next to me on the couch. Not really abnormal. The Braves were playing the Pirates. Rick Camp on the hill for Atlanta.

Next . . . the question that changed everything.

"Trey, have you walked to Hanky-Panky without letting me know?"

A heart rate rises when an animal — or a person — is threatened. How exactly was I threatened here?

"No. Why do you ask, Gran?"

"You sure? I know we have an agreement, that you don't stray beyond Cumberland Avenue without an adult. You're a big boy, Trey, but this is a big town, too." Orange County had nothing on Cleveland, Tennessee, not in Gran's eye. Dangers were real. And she was solely responsible for Libby and me.

"No, I haven't. I only go with you." Sealed. A lie might slip once. But two denials in the same conversation? I may as well have been branded, right there on Gran's couch. Game hadn't even reached the third inning.

"Well." Gran took a breath, smiled slightly. "I just don't understand. How did you know how to get to that corner store so well, if you'd never gone that route before?"

65

She didn't so much as give me time to crawl into the hole I was digging in what was once the foundation of my innocence. And that Brown Cow — now half-melted down my left arm – made its way to the trash bin. A heart rate indeed rises when an animal is threatened, and for good reason. An appetite, on the other hand, diminishes. There would be no dessert tonight. Gran was washing the dishes. Someone for the Pirates drove in the first run of the game with a triple. And for the first time in my life, I began to punish myself.

Lying in bed, shortly after 9:00, the tears began. If there was a saint in my life, it was Gran. A person who would allow the choice of her arms in exchange for my happiness. A person who would take as many trips to Hanky-Panky — via the route of my choosing — as I demanded. A person who planned her years now around the three months she was able to spend with me and my sister. Deceiving Gran hadn't been enough. I'd lied to her. And the punishment, of course, was that she knew it.

One day, Trey Milligan. The next . . . another Larry Blackwell.

* * *

Gran was watching *Knot's Landing* when I staggered back into the den, cheeks wet, eyes stinging, heart squeezed painfully tight.

"I'm sorry, Gran. I won't do it again. I promise."

The hug of a grandparent helps shape a soul. But when that hug is given out of genuine, unconditional love — really unconditional — it helps turn a boy into a man. When forgiveness is part of the wrapped arms, and understanding takes shape in the form of a gentle pat on the shoulder blades, you can actually feel your spirit cleansed. And mine was getting an ultra-wash on this night.

"I love you, Trey. You're the finest grandson in the world." Again, cleansing. Deep. "There aren't many rules here at Gran's house. But the ones we come up with, we have to follow. Don't you agree?"

Lips tight. Nod firmly. Try not to cry anymore.

"I never went alone, Gran. Always with Larry." The moment had been a perfect picture of cross-generational healing . . . until those last three words.

"That doesn't help, Trey. Larry Blackwell and his kin have their own rules. Some match ours, others don't. Make sure you remember and recognize the ones that don't. A stroll to Hanky-Panky, young man, doesn't match our rules."

I leaned in for another hug, this one lengthy. And I kept my mouth closed.

9

The Cleveland Fairgrounds was an under-used complex on the southern edge of town, built primarily for beer-league softball. It had two fields, a playground (where kids could be left out of the way of foul balls and spilled suds), a concession stand no more than twice the size of a toll booth, and a huge parking lot. Built to accommodate more than twice the number of cars it actually drew on softball nights, the lot actually served a critical role in Cleveland life.

This was where the kids of Cleveland High came on weekend nights to learn how to drink beer and steam up a windshield. Cleveland police, I later learned, actually helped pay for the oversized lot, convinced that underage drinking was a way of life, and if it could be contained at the Fairgrounds, there'd be considerably less detective work. And safer kids.)

Ironically, the Fairgrounds lost its intended purpose when the popularity of slow-pitch softball exploded in the late Seventies. Chattanooga had a complex with no fewer than eight fields, with teams playing five nights a week. Spring, summer, and fall. So the dozen or so teams from Cleveland that would have called the Fairgrounds home began traveling to Chattanooga for what they considered the big leagues. Made for some dusty dugout benches in Cleveland.

Two events remained that made the Fairgrounds the center of the universe each year. The Cleveland Carnival was held on Labor Day weekend, and drew vendors from Atlanta, Nashville, the Carolinas even. A Ferris wheel went up for the three-day event, along with a few kiddie rides.

I never actually attended the Cleveland Carnival, but I heard stories — from Larry every summer, less often from Devon — about Two-Tongue Tonya, the legendary "freak" who had been a mainstay at the Carnival in the Fifties and Sixties. According to legend, Tonya had — you guessed it — two tongues. And the tongues would move independently of one another, like a pair of serpents battling for supremacy in this poor woman's mouth. Carnival-goers would pay (Larry said five dollars; Devon claimed it was fifty cents) to enter a windowless boxcar and walk by Tonya, with a guarantee that she would "unleash her twin terrors."

Gran dismissed the tale and said she never — not once — set foot in that boxcar. Furthermore, she explained Tonya as merely being "what happens sometimes in Kentucky." That was then . . . a long time ago.

The other big event at the Fairgrounds — and the only other occasion when the light towers built for softball would be illuminated —. was the Fourth of July fireworks show. Gran took Libby and me each of our summers in Cleveland, and I grew to love the holiday more one year after the next. Because Wendy was there. And with her baseball glove.

Fireworks night at the Fairgrounds was the only time Cleveland ever felt crowded. The grand, oversized parking lot was actually full. (And not steamy windows.) Traffic cones extended parking lanes onto the outfield of one of the softball fields, one of Cleveland's finest directing late arrivals into their appropriate spot, facing what would have been the rightfield foul line.

In addition to the measly concession stand (candy bars, peanuts, and boxed popcorn that was impossible to chew), a Budweiser truck sold beer to thirsty parents and what Gran called "the big kids." And a traveling vendor — cleverly called "Fair Fare" — served up funnel cakes and pronto pups, making Cleveland's Fourth of July an official southern extravaganza.

Despite the expanded parking and the fireworks equipment taking up one of the two infields, there was plenty of grass for picnic blankets and hyperactive kids like Larry Blackwell. Larry spent the hours leading up to the fireworks menacing those reclining on blankets with "poppers," tiny quasi-firecrackers that, when thrown to the ground — and it took some effort on grass – would pop just loudly enough to startle. The playground filled with kids for Libby to chase (kids just as willing to chase her), five swings creating a mesmerizing, almost hypnotic display of life in motion. Those waiting for an available swing would pile landlocked sandcastles as high as a watered-down sandbox would allow. (The Budweiser truck would give us melted buckets of ice to water that box down, but good.)

As for "the big kids," they'd lean on cars, parked as far away as the Fairgrounds' fenced boundary would allow. The brazen would drink from plastic bottles filled with their favorite firewater. (Years later I came to wonder — after discovering some of that firewater myself — why anyone would want to see a fireworks display through blurred vision.) Judas Priest could be heard from the stereo of a football star's Mustang. Van Halen from that of a nearby Pinto.

But Jerry Nickerson always started his Fourth of July with Wendy, in the outfield grass, playing catch. To this day, I don't know if I was ever as cool with my younger sister as Jerry was with his on

Independence Day. Because it doesn't get any cooler than playing catch.

All it takes is two mitts and a baseball. And two people ready for an unexpressed intimacy that can't be found in any other endeavor. Jerry and Wendy may not have recognized it at the time. And I didn't recognize it with my dad all those times we played catch, in whichever backyard we called our own at the time. But I recognized it on the Fourth of July in 1982.

When words are hard to come by, you'll be amazed by what those two mitts and a baseball can do. Playing catch forces two people to share focus (unless you want a black eye), to take turns, to pause, and to, yes, look at one another. Whether it's from a distance of twenty feet or a hundred feet, the tossing of a ball between two people is an intimate act, and in such a way only two people with open hearts can fully appreciate. Feeling the slap of cowhide to leather when the ball is caught properly in a glove's pocket . . . is perfection. Likewise, drilling that hard, threaded sphere chest-high so that it causes a slap of its own . . . is perfection. And perfection is hard to come by, no matter the relationship.

Jerry finished tossing with Wendy when Julie DeMartin — that was his girlfriend; they were "Jerry and Julie" for three years at Cleveland High —

sauntered up and grabbed his throwing hand. Wendy knew when her turn with Jerry was over. And I made sure — for the third straight summer — I was in position to fill a void.

"Trey! Get over here and throw with Wendy," Jerry shouted. Having spent the last twenty minutes sitting no more than 20 yards away, glove at my side, I couldn't have been more obvious had I actually been stretching my right arm for action. "Show her that California arm of yours. And no necking behind the dugout."

It's hard to see a kid blush at dusk.

"Where's Larry?" she asked.

"Haven't seen him yet. I know he'll be here. Loves to see things explode, especially live."

Pop. Wendy could throw a baseball. And the sound when her toss hit my glove was the same as the one my teammates back in California made. It was a welcome sound, after so many hours in Gran's back yard, hearing a rubber ball settle more gently into my mitt.

"What position do you play?" Wendy knew I played Little League, and clearly knew the way to my heart with her line of questioning.

"Mostly first base last season." (I was tall for my age, remember.) "But I'm hoping to play centerfield next year. That's where I belong." The position mastered so elegantly by Willie Mays. Before him, Joe DiMaggio. Ten years was all it should take for me to assume the spot in St. Louis. I'd be 23 by then and have plenty of minor-league seasoning under my belt.

Pop. "My favorite position is second base. Easy throw to first, and you get to turn a double-play." Wendy didn't play baseball formally; the Cleveland little league didn't allow girls to play. But second is where her family put her when they had reunions. It was an easy throw, but she'd been making it since she was in second grade. She was a better second baseman than Todd Jackman, the kid who manned the position for my team — the Red Sox — back home.

And let me tell you: Wendy was a *lot* nicer to look at than Todd Jackman. Wearing her Hank Aaron t-shirt — number 44 prominent on the back — and blue jeans, she was beauty on that Fourth of July. She didn't wear a cap, didn't wear barrettes. Her straight, dirty-blonde hair would flop into her eyes with every throw she made, sometimes a little grunt giving the toss an extra push.

Pop. "Too bad we couldn't play for the same team. We'd be on the same side of the infield." As if I'd be able to concentrate on the hitter — much less a batted ball — with Wendy Nickerson standing in uniform, 40 feet to my right.

"Yeah, that would be cool. I'd scoop any low throws you made."

Pop. "I don't make low throws, Trey. Sometimes high, but never low."

We kept tossing as the sun escaped, under the field lights that illuminated this rare crowd at the fairgrounds. I had never played ball under the lights, so as Wendy and I played catch — pop following pop — fantasies merged, one with me playing among the same false shadows my Cardinal heroes knew, the other with me occupying Wendy's undivided focus for what seemed like an eternity and merely a stolen breath at the same time. It was fun.

"There's Devon!" Wendy had spotted him, winding his bike through cars in the parking lot. That orange paint job helped at this time of night. "Why did he ride his bike here?"

"I think he put it in his parents' trunk, actually. They wouldn't let him ride at night . . . except here." The guy loved that bike. It was as much a part of Devon McGee's summer as my Cardinal hat was mine.

Pop. "You better let him know where we are, Trey."

"Yeah. Here, I'll go get him." Pop.

10

Despite his size — and the color of his bike — Devon McGee was cool. He was cool because he didn't seem to *need* to be cool. To begin with, he was comfortable on his own. Particularly when he was riding through our neighborhood, pumping his pedals, yanking the front wheel up in the closest thing to an extended wheelie I'd seen by anyone under the age of 15. Devon was comfortable in his own skin, as they say, and that carried extra weight, he being among a select few black kids in Cleveland. He was great company whenever we played together, but he never demanded company to be happy. This made him cool to me.

"Hey, McGee!"

He wheeled around a row of cars parked on the edge of the paved lot, onto the grass, and back toward me, not acknowledging my greeting until he'd come to a stop five feet in front of me.

"Where's your ball, Milligan?"

"I was tossing with Wendy. She's here; let's go find a spot near the stage." The stage was the closest human beings could get to the launch site for the fireworks. Very decent chance a spark would land in your hair if you watched from near the stage.

"I knew it, Trey. You always find Wendy and her mitt on the Fourth. Smart boy, if you'd only been given a backbone." He got off his bike and started walking — bike at his side — with me through the crowd.

"Are your folks here?" I asked.

"Nah. Not their thing." I heard this a lot when it came to barbecues, pool parties, or big events like this. They just weren't the McGees' "thing." They were as friendly as any grown-ups I knew, from the West Coast to east Tennessee. But they were shy when it came to crowds. Took me a few years to consider some of the reasons for their timidity.

"You know the best thing about fireworks, Trey?"

"Volume! You can't hear yourself fart!"

"No, no. That's too easy, man. 'Volume!' he says. You're like a dog when he sees his dish filled, Trey. Gimme, gimme, gimme!

"The best thing about fireworks is that they're beyond our reach. Something you can only enjoy if you're a certain distance away. Unless you like blowing your fingers off or setting your hair on fire. Blackwell might get off on that."

Like I said, Devon was cool. And he said cool things.

"Hey Devon." Wendy handed me my baseball as she joined us, me now walking between two of the best friends I'll ever have for one of the last times.

"Trey said you hurt his hand, Wendy. Better not throw too hard with him. He's a Cardinal fan, remember." I always resented this stance. Devon wouldn't so much as claim a team, but took joy in tearing mine down.

"You know California boys throw like girls," cracked Wendy. I was taller than each of these people, but with a sense of humor not remotely close. "At least he can catch."

"LADIES AND GENTLEMEN OF CLEVELAND." One of the city aldermen was on stage, which means the show was about to begin. "WELCOME TO THE ANNUAL FOURTH OF JULY FESTIVAL! BEFORE WE GET STARTED, WE'D LIKE TO THANK JIMMY DEAN SAUSAGES AND COCA-COLA FOR SPONSORING OUR EVENT. THOSE OF YOU IN VEHICLES, PLEASE TURN OFF YOUR LIGHTS. AND PLEASE RISE FOR THE PLAYING OF OUR NATIONAL ANTHEM."

I've come to believe *The Star-Spangled Banner* is played too often. There are people who'd like to have me deported north of Canada for suggesting such, but I happen to believe this, and don't mind saying. The more you see a great movie, the less impact it has on you. The more you see a beautiful girl, the less you appreciate the details that make her so pretty.

(This had much to do with my feelings for Wendy, particularly over the nine months I didn't get to see her every year.) And the more you hear a song, the less real meaning it has.

Take a look sometime at the next ballgame you attend, and watch people during the national anthem. Some will stand attentive, holding their hats at their side, sometimes a hand over their heart. Others look as bored as they would in line at the department of motor vehicles. Standing to honor their country has become an obligation, not so much the act of respect it should be.

Save *The Star-Spangled Banner* for the World Series. For All-Star games and the Super Bowl. For Presidents' Day, Pearl Harbor Day, and September 11th. And save it for the Fourth of July. When I hear it now, I make myself think of the Fourth of July, especially those I spent in Cleveland.

And Devon was absolutely right that night. Those gorgeous explosions, with all their color, the streaming light brightening the black night, even after all the field lights had been shut off . . . they were beyond our reach. Twenty minutes of staring heavenward — oooooooohing and aaaaaaahing with the most impressive displays — forgetting that we were young or old, from Cleveland or elsewhere. Just that we were among friends, and under a spectacle.

* * *

On quiet days — like the 5th of July — my thoughts often turned to Granddaddy. He died in 1979, the year before Libby and I started summering in Cleveland. Complications from surgery after a diagnosis of colon cancer. The only exposure to mortality I'd had until Granddaddy's passing was the death of Elvis Presley, and that somehow felt like the end of a comic-book hero. Not the kind of impact I felt when I returned to Cleveland without a grandfather.

Strangely, what I remember most about Granddaddy are his whiskers. Not that he ever grew a beard, which is precisely why I remember the whiskers. Every morning, you see, Granddaddy would let me rinse his shaved whiskers from the sink in the master bathroom.

Some black, some gray, they looked like a spilled cup of salt and pepper, some lifted from the basin by the remnants of Granddaddy's shaving cream. Seeing those whiskers gently swirl down the drain as I poured a cup — and another cup — of water over the pattern was how my days started in Cleveland. And they were happy days, particularly when Granddaddy was nearby.

Frank Earl Johnson — as many people called Granddaddy by his middle name as did his first — was an alcoholic. Not that he so much as looked at a drop of liquor in the ten years I knew him, but Granddaddy was an alcoholic. He knew it, and was open with his grandchildren about it. ("Trey, your granddaddy is 22 years sober today.") Among my happiest memories with Granddaddy were trips to Alcoholics Anonymous meetings. These were among my grandfather's closest friends, so why wouldn't he want to show me off? Discussion would take its usual form at such gatherings, new men — only men at these meetings — would be welcomed, and I'd read comic books or color a picture at a table set aside just for me. All that mattered was Granddaddy was near. At the end of these meetings, when the group was offered "chips" for sobriety milestones, I'd always raise my hand. Blue, red, white . . . it didn't matter. Those little plastic disks were souvenirs of my trip with Granddaddy.

My grandfather came of age during the Great Depression. The oldest of six siblings, he left school after 5th grade to support his family, as his father had left, unable to do so himself. He clerked in grocery stores, apprenticed as an auto mechanic, labored in a paper mill, and finally turned to the moving business, where he first earned a salary, as opposed to an hourly wage. I learned of Granddaddy's youth only from my mother, who filtered the messy nights, the loud nights when her father drank his fatigue and worries aside. The bruises — physical or otherwise — had long faded by the time I became Granddaddy's running buddy. Alcoholism was simply a "bad-guy" defeated by another hero of mine, not unlike Spider-Man again disrupting a plot by the nefarious Green Goblin. "Who has earned a chip this week?" My grandfather was earning chips every day of his life.

On certain mornings — I'm still not sure how they were chosen — I'd rise before the sun with Granddaddy and go to work with him at the warehouse he managed in nearby Dalton, Georgia. On these mornings when the dew dampened my sneakers, I remember the smell of Granddaddy's cologne, almost as sweet as the aroma of his coffee, a brew he'd bring with him in a thermos for the hour-long ride to work.

I never felt more safe than I did in proximity to the recovering alcoholic that was Frank Earl Johnson. When he died, I was 10 years old, and my only thoughts of death had been when Elvis Presley suddenly left our world in my dad's hometown of Memphis, Tennessee. Elvis' death felt like fiction, as Elvis — to me — was in the realm of Spider-Man or

Batman. Only someone you see in books or on TV. But when Granddaddy died, I lost a real hero. As Gran later explained it to me (her version), he simply didn't wake up one morning. The nightly steaks and potatoes gave Granddaddy the belly he proudly patted when we'd watch baseball games together. Remember, he knew poverty in its scariest form. But such a diet squeezed his heart as tightly as his arms would squeeze me when we said goodbye. To this day, I feel like Granddaddy died from simply being too tired. I miss him. Not as much as Gran did — especially when Libby and I couldn't be there — but I miss him, to this day.

11

"Can I borrow Trey, Cooper? We need to set fire to this town, get good and drunk!" If Gran — and before her, Granddaddy — personified stability in my early life, Herb Wilbury was my wild card, the element beyond a child's understanding, a man who somehow mixed joy, fear, anxiety, and enthusiasm into a cocktail of confused emotion that likely hurt as much as it helped my summer days in east Tennessee.

"Don't talk that way, Herb. It wasn't funny when Frank was alive. It's not funny now." Gran tolerated her nephew, but barely.

And yes, Herb was Gran's nephew. Remember, Gran had ten older siblings. Best I could tell, Herb was older than my grandmother . . . but Gran's nephew. Seems perfectly Southern when I look back. Only confused me when I was 13.

"Aw, Cooper. That child is way too straight. He needs some roughin' up, some whiskey on his boots, and a good-lookin' woman cookin' his ham and eggs!"

Herb was all show. He was an entertainer. A horse trainer by day (and yes, a heavy drinker by night when he wasn't having dinner at Gran's), Herb Wilbury aimed for laughs wherever he was, and he typically got them.

Once or twice each summer, Herb would come "retrieve" me for what he called Man Time. Since Granddaddy died, he was concerned that too many weeks surrounded by my grandmother and sister would turn me into what he called a "light-footed fancy." Which was hardly the worst I might be called by Herb. In addition to being brilliant around horses — these were the days before "horse whisperer" became part of the lexicon around stables — and sloppy around liquor, Herb was an unfiltered and unapologetic racist.

"Them sand-niggers can't govern themselves," he'd say. "Ain't oil that's the problem, and it ain't all crazy, because there AIN'T NO WATER IN THE DESERT!"

What made Herb's brand of racism especially scary was the fuel he gained by actually reading the newspaper. If a plane went down piloted by a man named Callahan, then "no Mick can fly a jet airplane . . . it's a proven fact, right here on page five." And yes, he'd tell this to a boy named Milligan.

"Pinkos want to rule the world." Herb had a particular distaste for the Soviet Union, having come of age during what those younger and more educated came to know as the Cold War. "But you see, there ain't no system that can make one man think like another. Hasn't worked here; just look at all the bitchin' in Washington. The slopes can't make it happen in China or Japan, and they actually wear suits in Tokyo and manufacture a car cheaper than Detroit. You just can't make two men think alike. So how does some Vodka-swillin' Russian think he's gonna make ten million commies share money, business, manufacturing. Hell, they'd have women distributed by quota if they could!"

This was ugly talk, and Herb knew his audience. My father — working toward his Ph.D., aiming to become a man of the world — was uncomfortable with the language, but laughed under his grimace, seeing a nugget of truth (however miniscule) in Herb's hateful rants. On the days I spent with Herb, my elder cousin became a preacher to a flock of one. I managed to listen long enough for us to shift the conversation to baseball. Herb was a Cardinal fan, too.

"He needs to be home for supper, Herb." Gran trusted me with a whiskey-loving racist who owned several guns — we'll get to them soon — but not when it came to feeding me. "And if you want a pork chop tonight, you can join us. Six o'clock."

"Let's go, Trips."

86

Herb liked calling me Trips. Confused me mightily the first ten years of my life. "If we ain't trapped in some Chattanooga whorehouse, we'll be here for pork chops with your grandma. Grab your mitt, and let's go."

I had one grown-up to play catch with during my summers in east Tennessee, and I never missed the chance.

Herb lived on a farm he inherited from his father (one of Gran's older brothers), not far from Etowah, where my mom was raised. He and his second wife, Maggie, had a two-story, white clapboard house with dark-green shutters. A pair of magnolias flanked the long driveway that took you to the front, then around to the side of the house.

From the side, you could see into the field behind Herb's home, where as many as a dozen horses would graze. The stables ran perpendicular to the screened back porch of the house, about 100 yards across the field. Beyond the field, nothing but woods. To a city boy who had known Atlanta and Los Angeles, Cleveland, Tennessee felt like a getaway. But Herb Wilbury's farm felt like the end of the earth.

"You're ridin' Freckles today, Trips. She ain't been exercised in weeks. Fella your size will do her good."

Fact is, I was afraid of horses. Any animal larger than my Labrador retriever back home was a threat in my eyes. But on visits with Herb, I found my faith in his training skills outweighed my fear of being thrown by one of these big, gorgeous creatures.

"Is she good?" I didn't know how to measure "good" in a horse, but I knew Herb did. "Does she run?" By "run," I meant, "Will she take off, hop the fence and gallop across three counties before I have my heart attack?"

"She ain't gonna buck ya, Trips! Just let 'er know ya love her. Horses are like women, the good ones anyway. The good women. Pat 'em the right way, feed 'em, give 'em a good bath now and then, and let 'em know who's boss . . . and they'll be yours forever."

I never found out which of these rules Herb broke with his first wife. They had two daughters — Mary Ann and Celia — who grew up to win show-jumping competitions from Richmond to Atlanta, and all over Tennessee.

Mary Ann was my first idea of female beauty. Long, straight brown hair, skin a color that seemed to match the chestnut horses she rode so elegantly. They'd both grown up and married, though. I didn't get to see them all that much on my summer visits.

When Herb put me on a horse, he did so as if he

were loading bales of hay in his pickup. Once on the horse — today, Freckles — I'd cling to the animal as though I were 10 stories above terra firma. Just as I swam merely to keep from drowning, I rode horses as the more attractive alternative to falling off. Now, I heard Herb's instructions: "Heels down! Squeeze yer legs, Trips. Squeeze 'em tight! Back up, boy! Gotta be straight in the saddle." I heard the instructions, but I was just hanging on.

Herb was of a generation that connected a man's hair to oil. Long before mousse or "gels" became part of a man's medicine cabinet, oil was used to keep a gentleman — or even Herb Wilbury — properly coiffed. Just into his fifties, Herb's hair was still primarily brown, and with it combed tightly to his scalp, he didn't look all that different from the salesmen who would help me try on shoes at Caldwell's Department Store. But with blue jeans and boots — Herb's "ass-kickers," as he called them — he belonged outside. The way he squinted in the sunshine — Herb would no sooner wear sunglasses than he would a tattoo — gave him a look I associated with Clint Eastwood. Still do.

"You gotta post, Trips. She can feel your tension, little man. You ride *with* a horse, not on a horse." I wanted to be able to post, to become one with my steed. The best I could do, though, was to maintain

89

the asymmetrical route — couldn't call it a circle — around my oiled-up, gutter-mouthed horse whisperer.

Herb spoke to his horses more than anyone in a saddle. But it wasn't English, not even Herb-ese. Just a series of clicks, whistles, and grunts. He never shouted. I also never saw Herb Wilbury so much as slap a horse with his hand in anger. Looking back now, it's clear he felt a kinship to the equine species in ways he never did with other human beings. A redeeming quality, perhaps.

"I'm slipping, Herb. Can't hold on much longer!" The only way I could end the session was to act like I was ceding control, as though I ever had it in the first place. The one skill I mastered was a gentle tug on the reins, the universal signal for a horse to slow down. Freckles was a good horse. Never let me know how weak a rider I actually was.

"Attaboy, Trips. We'll make you a cowboy yet. Pat 'er on the hind quarters. See if your hand gets wet."

The muscle on the rear end of a horse is unmatched in the animal kingdom. Beautiful in movement, the bundle of muscles seem to want to explode from underneath Freckles' skin. And yep, she was sweating. My hand was damp after I patted her.

"Saddest thing on earth, Trips, is a horse that don't get run. They need to run like we need a cold drink in July. You did a good thing today, boy."

"Thanks, Herb. She's a sweet horse. Did Mary Ann ride her?"

"We got Freckles a year or two after Mary Ann moved to Nashville. She's been on 'er, but not in competition."

"I bet they'd be a good pair."

"Mary Ann made a good pair with just about every horse she rode." That was as sentimental as Herb would ever get. Combine his daughters and horses, and you actually discovered Herb's soft spot.

"Let's get you a cheese dog. The way you rode today, I just might let you try the cold beer this time."

He was always joking about the beer. Never made me comfortable with the talk, though. What would Granddaddy say?

* * *

"Your grandma tells me you're playing baseball with them surfers. I didn't know folks in California took time away from the beach long enough to learn how to hit a cowhide."

"Yeah, I played for the Red Sox this year. We went 12-8."

Herb and I talked baseball as he prepared his

specialty: fried cheese dogs. He'd slit a foot-long hot dog down the middle, throw it on a frying pan till the grease oozed over and around the blackened edges of the slit. Then just before removing it from the pan, Herb would place a narrow slice of cheddar cheese into the slit. Not a lunch any physician would recommend, but a taste I'll forever associate with visits to Herb's farm.

"What position?"

"I played a lot of first base; some outfield." Again, I was among the tallest kids in my class . . . thus the first base assignment. While grounders could eat me up, I handled a fly ball rather well. Thus, the outfield.

"Sounds like you're a slugger, Trips. First base and outfield is where you find a team's power. Johnny Mize, Stan the Man, Enos Slaughter."

Wouldn't help for me to remind my Cardinal-loving cousin that Rogers Hornsby was a second-baseman and quite a slugger. Or that Ernie Banks was a shortstop and hit more than 500 home runs. Heck, he was complimenting me, having never seen me flail at a curve ball.

Herb's kitchen was small — a "step-saver" he liked to call it — but he made up for it with the biggest living room/dining room in four counties.

We ate our cheese dogs at his dining table (large

enough to seat eight, but rarely with a crowd larger than we had on this July afternoon). You entered this grand space through a swinging door from the kitchen. Once seated you could stare out through space no longer encumbered by a wall that originally separated the two rooms. And staring right back at you, from a distance of about 30 yards, was Thorny.

Mounted above a fireplace Herb and Maggie hardly ever used was what remained of a gorgeous buck. Herb liked to say a hunter becomes a full-time fisherman when he turns 50. Well, Thorny was the prize of Herb's previous avocation. There wasn't another hint of taxidermy in this farmhouse, but Thorny had been there as long as I could remember. Snout slightly raised, all eight points of his antlers sharp enough to pierce a can of corn. Thorny seemed to be saying, "He may have got me in this life, but we'll meet again."

Thorny was only one of the reasons, by the way, that Gran never let Libby come with me to Herb's place . . . at least not without coming herself. The first time Libby saw Thorny — she was still in diapers — she cried all the way back to Gran's house. And she wouldn't sleep in her own room for six nights. Gorgeous trophy to one man, blood-curdling slice of death to a little girl. I could never have pulled the trigger Herb did on Thorny's last day, but I always found him more beautiful than revolting.

"It's good your folks send you back home every summer, Trips." East Tennessee would always be "home" to Herb, and he attached the same comforts to me, even though I'd already lived in Europe a year and two more in California. "Your grandma, she wouldn't show it, but she's been lonely since Frank died. Friends are one thing, but they ain't family. Family knows where you been, and usually where you're goin'."

"Libby and I like it here." No exaggeration there. "The days seem to slow down, and I don't mind. Helps not to have homework or practice schedules."

"You hurl that rubber ball in the backyard, though, to keep your arm strong, dontcha?"

"Yeah. Not sure if I'll ever be a pitcher, but it helps me with grounders."

"Listen, Trips. I hope you grow up to be a Cardinal." This was either a new and backdoor way of Herb's presenting his "let's-get-drunk" proposal, or he was getting serious . . . and without a horse nearby.

"But you follow your daddy's path; your mama's, too. They got more diplomas than most folks have hats. But the fancy paper on the wall ain't nothin' more than a symbol. It's the learnin' your folks have done that has steered 'em right. The books

94

they've read, the questions they've asked when it's time to ask questions. Me, I had to be home with enough sunlight left to clean stables. That was my direction. Wasn't legal to skip school, or I'd a skipped it every day." (Herb left Etowah High School for the last time as a sophomore, just after he turned 16.)

"What I'm tellin' ya, is that I admire your daddy. He sure did right when he fell ass-over-kettle for your mama. I'm grateful that we get to chase women together every summer, but follow their lead, Trips." Herb wasn't squinting anymore, but the creases in his face — caused by more than merely aging — kept him in that Eastwood category. I can see that face when I remember him today. It was the last time Herb Wilbury ever told me he admired my parents. Never did tell them personally.

12

The last time I played with Devon McGee felt like an average day at Gran's. All that stands out now, thirty years later, is an ice cream truck, an uncomfortable conversation with Arline, and the fact that it was an unspoken goodbye to one of my best friends.

Mornings were lazy, as summer mornings should be. Gran usually cooked some bacon, ready on the kitchen table when I woke up around eight o'clock, maybe eight-thirty. I'd butter some toast, drink a glass of milk, and before the dew had dried on the backyard grass — what my pitching and fielding had left of it — I headed out for a game of one-man baseball. I wasn't so much trying to beat the oven-like heat of midday; it was just the best way I knew to start a summer day. With a mitt on my left hand, and visions of Busch Stadium in my mind.

I usually found my way back inside Gran's air-conditioned sanctuary by ten o'clock, for the first of two *Three's Company* reruns. It was the perfect comedy for a 13-year-old boy: sexual allusions that filled in some of the mysterious blanks of puberty (all the better with Suzanne Somers occupying a few of the blanks), but with the most elementary of comedic devices (the misunderstood conversation).

Devon showed up as the second episode was starting. He never called, but his parents didn't allow him to watch *Three's Company* at his house. He was smart enough not to make for Gran's place too early, but knew quite well a full episode awaited if he could get to Gran's den by 10:30. (The McGees and Gran had differing approaches to censorship. My 8-year-old sister knew Jack Tripper like a second brother. Libby had no idea what the big fuss was over being "gay." She considered her best friends gay, and so included John Ritter's character among her favorites on TV.)

"Is Chrissy in this one?" Devon had a few beads of sweat on his forehead, and no time for greetings with our show under way. Devon considered it a scandal along the lines of Watergate when Jenilee Harrison replaced Somers. He never understood it, and I didn't try.

"She's trying to cook something with Jack. But Roper's in the other room." Such was basically every episode of *Three's Company*. The operative word was "cooking." Only a matter of what — or who — was on the menu.

"You wanna ride?" Devon would interrupt his adventures on wheels for only a few distractions,

Suzanne Somers being one of them. Ballgame and blondes already behind me, I hopped on the dusty hand-me-down Gran kept in her utility closet, and Devon and I rode.

"You think Chrissy would like a black man?" Devon had asked this before, and the only answer I could give was the one I gave today.

"She'd like a cool black man over a white dweeb, absolutely. Now, if the black man acted like Jack Tripper, that's another story."

"Would you date a black girl, Trey? I mean a *fine* black lady. Would you?"

Considering the closest thing to a date I'd known was the infamous Braves-Phillies game in Arline's trailer, how could I answer a question like this?

"If she's fine, and she likes me . . . why not? But I wouldn't date an ugly black girl just to prove a point."

"That's where I'm different from you, Trey. I just might date an ugly white girl. To prove a point."

"Just to prove that a black guy can date a white girl?"

"No. To prove that what you see isn't always what you get. Whether someone's white or black — or whether they're good lookin' or butt-ugly — we expect one picture, the same picture. And I wouldn't mind proving that sometimes the picture changes, right in front of you."

"Man, I can't see you riding that precious bike of yours anywhere near an ugly chick. You'd be afraid that orange paint would crack."

Devon laughed; laughed so hard his bike swerved. And Devon's bike rarely swerved.

* * *

If fireworks exploding over the Fairgrounds are the indelible image from summers in Cleveland, the jingle of an ice-cream truck is the sound I can still hear in rare moments of silence. The truck was driven by a black woman who seemed large enough to fill both front seats. (This may be because I never saw anyone in that rolling fridge with her.) Geraldine was her name.

One of Geraldine's two upper front teeth was gold, and the sparkle off that tooth when she smiled was as much a part of her greeting as the metallic melody that called kids from every house or playground within earshot. It wasn't until I was in college that I learned "When the Saints Go Marching In" had a spiritual element, that the song means more than fudgsicles, push-up pops, and nutty buddies.

Devon and I had looped around the neighborhood, almost back to Gran's, when we heard Geraldine's truck and spotted her down Woodward Avenue, at rest in the middle of Arline's trailer park.

"I'll get some money," I offered. "Meet you down there."

"Just come on, Trey. I've got some." Devon left his house prepared.

A line had already formed. Many kids I recognized from my infrequent visits to the community Arline called home. Adults were in line, too. (It's a myth that one outgrows the Ice Cream Man. Sort of like the myth of outgrowing your favorite cartoon.)

A pregnant woman was up front, apparently ordering for an entire brood.

"Gimme four of them rocket pops, a nutty buddy, and two chocolate-chip samiches."

"That's five dollars, honey. Now you get back home and off ya feet. That little one needs carin' for before he's out here runnin' around and hollerin'." There was a rumor — long told by Gran — that Geraldine had 11 kids. The rumor was told in a complimentary tone, as Gran was convinced she supported her family entirely with the sale of ice cream.

"I gotta have me a creamsicle, Trey. What do you want?"

I turned from the cartoonishly cluttered menu stickers on the truck's side just long enough to see the person I didn't necessarily want to see right then. Wearing cut-off jeans and a red tank top with Superman's logo, Arline strolled to the back of the line. The four people between us in line weren't nearly enough to form a buffer. It had been almost three weeks since that Braves-Phillies game, but it felt like three minutes ago.

"Hey there, Devon. Hey Trey." Did she acknowledge Devon first with a purpose? Were there others she romanced over milkshakes and the national pastime? Was I second-fiddle already?

"What's happenin' Arline?" Devon couldn't care less that the girl who tore down my wall of sexual boundaries was in our presence. But I couldn't talk. I really couldn't.

"Heh." That's all that came out.

"Whatcha gettin'?" Was she asking me? Or her "other" boyfriend? "Trey! Whatcha gettin'?"

"Heh."

"He's just getting a napkin, Arline. Needs to wipe that drool off his bottom lip."

The mystery here, was how Arline — knowing what she did, having *done* what she did — could act so casual in an ice-cream line. She hadn't seen me since The Kiss. She hadn't even spoken to me on the phone since The Kiss. (Three weeks without a phone call from her had been a record, for sure. And not until this very moment did I realize that I'd missed the calls. Wendy may have been on my mind every day . . . but Arline had managed to intrude.)

"Shut up, Devon. I know what I'm getting." I was never abrupt, unless Libby was on my last nerve or the Cardinals were losing. While I didn't know what to say to Arline, I sure didn't need Devon's ribbing at this transcendent moment in the ice-cream line.

"Boy, you need to remember who's buying here. Tellin' me to shut up. Do you hear the way Trey's talkin' to me, Geraldine?"

"Take it easy, fellas. There's enough to go around." Geraldine's wisdom seemed to describe 12-year-old girls as much as it did her frozen delights.

Finally at the front of the line. "I'll have a creamsicle," said Devon.

"What about you, Mr. California?" Geraldine thought California was exotic, and didn't pay attention to the fact I was born in Knoxville.

"I'll have a nutty buddy . . . please."

"Dollar-fifty . . . you boys stay cool. Don't be starin' at bikinis all summer."

102

I blushed. Ninety-five degrees outside, sun baking the layer of sweat that had formed on our bodies the minute we stepped outside. One mention of bikinis from this 250-pound ice cream queen, though, and I blushed. Devon had his opening.

"Man, what is wrong with you all of a sudden? You got the hots for Geraldine, don't you?!" Walking back to our bikes — still lying next to the drainage ditch on the side of the road — I stared straight ahead. Didn't look back. Devon's words were meant to tease me without hurting Geraldine.

I carefully removed the top of my nutty buddy. (Underneath the lid were loose nuts, treats you'd lose if you were haphazard in the way you tore the packaging. Lid first, then the wrap that descended around the cone.) "I don't have the hots for anyone, Devon. *Anyone,* okay? Maybe you have the hots for Geraldine, or that girl you talk to at the pool . . . Debbie? Yeah, you must have the hots for Debbie."

"My favorite will always be ice cream sandwiches." Arline's voice cracked the growing tension between Devon and me . . . and her presence, looking back, killed my taste buds for the next twenty minutes. The tension may have been cracked, but not Devon's wit.

"Ice cream sandwiches . . . yeah, they're tasty." Devon was now talking with a large bite of creamsicle melting in his mouth, glimpses of orange with every word he spoke. "Trey was just telling me about his favorite girls, Arline. He mentioned Geraldine."

"Don't be mean, Devon." Arline was smiling when she admonished my tormenter, but looking right at me . . . when I blushed again.

The trouble with ice cream — maybe the only trouble with ice cream — is that it's physically impossible to eat ice cream and ride a bike at the same time. Here we were, the three of us, basically trapped — ice cream melting on its way to our mouths — in a conversational club, no topic decided, and none off limits.

"Braves are playing better than they were that night, huh Trey?"

I could actually feel my pulse quickening, my heart thumping. Could Devon and Arline *see* my heart thumping? Was that visible under my Roger Staubach t-shirt?

"Yeah, I guess."

"Murphy hit two homers last night!"

On one level, Arline was the first woman in my life to recognize the way to my heart. Talking baseball put me at ease, erased worries, seemed to solve problems, even. But now? The path this girl had found to my heart was paved with anxiety.

Thank god it was so hot outside. The sweat on my brow looked like it belonged.

"What night are you talking about?," inquired Devon, a drip of orange tenderly working its way down his chin and toward his neck.

"Trey didn't tell you about the night we watched the Braves at my house?"

This was getting ugly, and fast.

"Naaah, nothing." Devon was ready to pounce. Worst part was, I saw it coming.

"Did you cook dinner, Arline?"

"No dinner . . . but we had milk shakes. Mom's specialty."

"Milk shakes . . . that's nice. No man can resist a good milk shake."

I should have dropped what was left of my nutty buddy — right there — and jumped on my bike. No ice cream was worth this round-about interrogation. Nothing was cold enough or sweet enough to reduce the fever I'd endure as long as Arline and Devon were together in this G-rated menage a trois. Escape, Trey! Escape!!

"You should come back, Trey. Braves and Cardinals next week."

"Yeah, maybe." This, of course, was the first time a female not named Milligan had so much as considered watching a Cardinal game with me. Years later, I'd consider such a gesture among the criteria for a wife. But in the summer of my 14th year, it was the kind of bait that would lead only to disaster. Arline may have presented the bait, but my best friend Devon was holding the rod and reel.

"You better bring flowers next time, Trey. You hear me?" Devon stifled his laugh for a breath or two, but then it came. A high-pitched cackle that seemed to rattle his teeth as it left him. Arline . . . she just smiled and stared directly at me.

I finally finished the longest ice-cream-cone I ever would eat. Devon and I picked up the bikes, turned back toward Gran's street, and rode off . . . not as fast as I would have liked. We didn't say goodbye to Arline, didn't so much as turn and wave. Rude. Childish. The way of boys eager to become men, but with no sense yet how to get there.

"Man, Arline likes you . . . a lot." Devon wasn't chuckling, didn't seem to be teasing as we neared Gran's driveway.

"What are you talking about? We watched a baseball game. No big deal. She's a kid!" For a 13-year-old boy, remember, a 12-year-old girl was, yes, a kid. Not yet familiar with the ways of junior high.

"She likes you, Trey." Why wasn't Devon riding home on that beloved orange bike? Why was he lingering? Heck, why was I lingering?

"Man, you need to focus on things you understand, and leave romance to the experts." Perhaps the only time in our friendship that I talked down to Devon McGee.

"I saw you blush, Trey. You like her, too. One of the cool things about being black is we don't blush. Farrah could kiss me on the cheek in front of a packed football stadium . . . and I'd be as cool as Marvin Gaye. Our blush is invisible. But you? With that pale Irish skin? You like her, too, Trey."

"I'm outta here. Gran's playing cards tonight. We've got a babysitter. I gotta take a shower."

"You do that, Milligan. I'll see ya. Remember something: love ain't about what you're thinkin'. And you may not be thinking about Arline Varden. Love's about what you're feelin'."

It was the last thing Devon McGee ever said to me. A gift I'll never forget, and one I can never repay.

13

Summers at Gran's were liberating . . . until card night came around. Once a month — so three times each summer — Gran would join seven or eight of her best friends at Wilma Bennett's place on the other side of town to play cards.

As much as she cherished the time she got to spend with Libby and me, she considered her card night sacred. This is a gathering that began after Granddaddy died, a social spark in Gran's otherwise quiet life.

Libby and I understood how much it meant to Gran, so we never griped when the special Friday appeared on the calendar. (Gran actually taped an ace of hearts on the date each month as her reminder.) And we didn't gripe — though I desperately wanted to — when Gran arranged for a babysitter.

In some ways, my grandmother Johnson recognized the man in me before anyone else. She didn't script my days, didn't assign chores, and never cited rules and regulations for life at her house. She allowed whatever maturity I might muster to surface naturally.

But Gran simply could not imagine a 13-year-old boy in charge of her house. Now, Libby had much to do with this, of course. A 13-year-old boy might be capable of holding down the fort a few hours on his own, but with an 8-year-old sister to care for? Not in Gran's eyes. Her call to the Dunham family was as automatic as that ace of hearts taped to the calendar.

Roger Dunham managed the supermarket where Gran had shopped for years, a Winn-Dixie just off the exit from I-75. Mr. Dunham always greeted Gran with a smile, even called her when fresh produce had arrived. Cleveland was getting bigger every year I visited, but Mr. Dunham and his supermarket were decidedly small-town.

Mr. Dunham had a pair of daughters, Karen and Rosemary. Rosemary — the younger by four years — had been our sitter each of the three summers Libby and I spent in Cleveland. With dirty blonde hair cascading past her shoulder blades, Rosemary was just this side of gorgeous. She was four years older than me, which may as well have been an entire generation during the time we knew each other. To her credit, she treated me like a friend, letting me stay up until I wanted to go to bed. (Gran had established a bedtime of 9:00 when she was out. Odd, because she never really enforced a bedtime when she was in.) Rosemary enlisted my help if Libby got upset about her own bedtime, but even managed to handle my sister's protests. All it took was a love story from the halls of Cleveland High School, tales Rosemary came up with — if, in fact, they were fiction — with the ease of a schoolteacher.

But on this night — the last card night I can remember, and the only one I'll never forget — Rosemary wasn't available to stay with us. Which meant her older sister, Karen, would be our housemate. And Karen was not Rosemary.

Karen had fallen in line with millions of girls in the late Seventies and early Eighties, a legion of ladies who felt Lynda Carter was the ideal female form. (Carter, of course, gained fame as Wonder Woman on a TV series that lasted at least three years longer than it should have.)

Karen was cursed, like her younger sister, in that she had blonde hair (a shade lighter than Rosemary's). But she wore it past her shoulders, and used curling irons to give it what she considered a "natural wave." She actually described her hair this way to Libby and me. "Hair color doesn't matter so much," she once emphasized. "It's the natural waves." We both *saw* her using her curling iron.

Like Diana Prince, Karen wore eyeglasses. Whether or not she needed them to see was incidental. (We never saw her crack a book.) But the big, brown frames accentuated her dime-store Wonder Woman impression. They seemed to say, "just imagine when I take these off." Tight blue jeans and a tan button-down blouse completed the Karen Dunham Look on this particular night. Her sense of aggravation at the idea of Libby and me being priorities wasn't so much implied as exuded.

Card night for Gran also meant TV dinner night. (Rosemary always brought Jiffy Pop popcorn. Not something we could count on with Karen.) TV dinners — always Swanson's — were a creation of the Fifties that somehow survived into the Eighties and beyond, dodging every health-food craze and mainstream diet with a standard impossible to duplicate.

Packaged in an aluminum tray that was heated — all four items at once — for about a half hour, a TV dinner was the culinary equivalent of Cliff's Notes: a quick, easy-to-digest (well . . .) summary of a person's nutritional needs. Gran's selection tended to be the same, one card night after another: fried chicken (two pieces), mashed potatoes, mixed vegetables, and apple pie.

The mashed potatoes were somehow injected with butter (or butter-tasting substance). Made them palatable. The chicken was okay. Always stuck to the aluminum tray, but once gently pulled away —

leaving a greasy scab hard to look at — a close proximity to the treats we had now and then at Kentucky Fried Chicken. The vegetables were a combination "platter" of peas, corn, and tiny carrot cubes. How carrots were cut and molded into tiny dice is a phenomenon still beyond me, but they joined their nutritional cousins in a mixture I would endure . . . and one Libby would transform (with the help of the potatoes) into artwork.

Libby's treatment of a TV dinner was deserved, really. Anything that held so tightly to formula should be given a twist. And a child's mind is capable of some violent twisting. My little sister managed to eat her apple pie — the smallest of the tray's four compartments, always top and center — without actually swallowing any part of an apple. She would peel back the crust (the only part I actually liked) and chew it like the dry-on-one-side cookie it was. She'd then find a spoon and manage to scoop up the brownish syrup of the pie, slurping it like Mary Poppins' proverbial spoonful of sugar. It was disgusting, but the child had a method. And you had to respect her for it.

As for the veggies, it was only a matter of what — or who — Libby could bring to life with some orange, green, and yellow on a canvas of semi-soft white potato. Peas might become a smile, with carrots the eyes, and yellow the bright blonde hair of our beloved Rosemary. One time, Libby actually designed a house — a floor plan! — with her mixed vegetables. I couldn't recognize it until she took me on a tour with her fork: a hallway of carrots, peas representing the bedrooms (three of them!), with corn forming the oversized bathrooms Libby gave more attention than she needed to. Gran had to see these creations when she took out the garbage the morning after card night. But she never brought it up. And Libby and I never went hungry.

A combination of TV dinner and — this being Friday night — *The Dukes of Hazzard* meant Karen's job was done. Once Libby and I were set up on the folding card table in the living room (irony there), Karen retired to Gran's bedroom in the back, where she could more privately talk on the phone with the young suitors of Cleveland, Diana Prince doing her best Wonder Woman voice impression.

Only 13, I didn't know a stereotype from stereo phones, so cheering the adventures of Bo and Luke Duke on Friday night seemed as natural — almost — as pulling for my Cardinals on a Sunday afternoon. Hazzard County may as well have been a few miles south of Cleveland, near the Georgia border. Boss Hogg was pure evil, even as he dressed in white from head to toe. Rosco P. Coltrane was the dimwitted sheriff, straight from some Robin Hood tale. And Daisy Duke . . . well, she's a stereotype I can handle to this day.

Every *Dukes* episode was the same. Bo and Luke would innocently visit someone in the nether reaches of Hazzard County (or if daring, cruise downtown — near the jail and courthouse! — in the General Lee). A misunderstanding would ensue, with "them Duke boys" guilty of one transgression or another. A big car chase, always on a dirt road. Usually a fist fight (no blood). Then a wrap-up in which Daisy would kiss one of the boys ("Awww, Daisy . . . if you wasn't my cousin!"), and Uncle Jesse would crack wise about the continued ineptitude of Boss Hogg. As Waylon Jennings sang, "Just the good ol' boys, never meaning no harm . . . ."

No network today could get away with making the American South look so numb-in-the-brain and incestuous. If there was a black man (or woman) who played a significant role in any *Dukes* adventure, I don't remember him (or her). But this show was a cartoon come to life for kids. Libby loved it as much as I did.

* * *

Bedtime for Libby was 9 o'clock. She knew *Dallas* — the prime-time soap opera that followed the *Dukes* — was off limits. Gran let me stay up and watch with her, and I told myself I understood all the misplaced romance and power struggles of the Ewing family. But it was really for a glimpse of Victoria Principal. Daisy Duke woke me up on Friday nights, but Pamela Ewing drew my attention.

With Libby tucked in — no thanks to Karen, still in Gran's bedroom, surely on the phone — the den was mine. Which meant I could invade Gran's Butterfinger stash without my little sister begging for her own late-night chocolate. My grandmother had two staples in her life: there was always frozen okra in the freezer, and there were always bite-sized Butterfingers in her dresser drawer.

At the first commercial break — J.R. was smiling devilishly over his latest decision, same as every first commercial break, it seemed — I strolled down the hallway and saw Gran's door all but closed. Karen wouldn't actually go to sleep, would she? No . . . the light was on, I could see through the crack in the doorway. So I opened the door . . . .

"TREEEEEEEY!!! GET OUT! OUT!!!!!"

Across Gran's bedroom, in front of her full-length mirror, stood Karen Dunham. Her back was to me. And she was wearing nothing but a bra and silk panties, both of them pink. Oh . . . she had her glasses on, too. My first R-rated night. Well, my first PG-13 night.

115

Karen saw me through the mirror, and never turned around, even as she did her best Fay Wray. She certainly saw me stand rigid with shock, surprise, and a small slice of glee. Not sure if I smiled; probably not. I had come to the back of the house merely for some chocolate, a 13-year-old boy with sweet tooth on a Friday night with no rules. But on the other side of my grandmother's bedroom door, I'd found . . . a woman. A woman apparently admiring what made her a woman. In context — Karen was babysitting my sister and me, for crying out loud — the scene was a major transgression. At the moment, though, it seemed to fill in a blank or two.

I'd spent six weeks looking at Wendy Nickerson differently than I had in summers past. I'd been kissed by Arline Varden during a televised baseball game, an event that became more thrilling as the summer wound its way toward August. But if any confusion remained in my junior-high brain over the differences between Wendy and me (or Arline and me), Karen Dunham managed to wipe it clear out of my consciousness in a moment that didn't last 30 seconds.

I closed the door. Tightly. I could hear Karen stomping around Gran's bedroom, surely retrieving her clothes. This was when the event got scary. How was she going to act when — once clothed again — she got out of Gran's bedroom? Hell, *how was I going to act?* Between pretending I saw nothing and addressing the confrontation honestly, I wasn't sure which made me more uncomfortable. At the moment I closed that door, though, I just hoped Gran was nowhere near her house.

Back in the den, I shut off the TV. No Pam Ewing sighting tonight . . . I'd had so much more. I didn't so much as brush my teeth before heading to my room, throwing on my pajamas — in the closet, just in case my door was suddenly thrown ajar — and crawling into bed. No baseball cards, no comics, no winding down. However Karen acted once outside her adopted nudist's sanctuary, it would be on her own. Trey Milligan was sound asleep. A story I already had written when my heart rate finally slowed again.

I woke up the next morning — a Saturday — and found Gran and Libby eating cereal in the kitchen. Apple Jacks for my sister, Special K for my grandmother, box on the counter, next to Gran's coffee pot, her dark-brown elixir dripping to the rhythm of a normal day's start.

"Morning, Trey," said Gran.

Libby had her Strawberry Shortcake doll on the table. Looked like it was holding an Apple Jack. Yep,

117

a normal day's start.

"Karen said you all had a good time last night. Said you mostly just watched TV."

"Yeah, we watched the Dukes."

"Does Karen like Bo or Luke? I know Rosemary has a crush on Bo."

"She didn't say, Gran. I'm not sure."

"Oh well. She was mighty nice to help us on short notice. Hopefully Rosemary will be back next month."

And the Naked Babysitter Incident — that's the title I give it today — ended just that quietly. I only saw Karen Dunham once more, and it was an occasion neither of us planned on attending, much less enjoy remembering. We shared a glance that day (I'll get to the story), and I recall Karen smiling slightly. Looking back, it was an understanding we reached. An unspoken understanding. And it was yet another important lesson from that summer. The secrets a man and woman are able to keep between each other are more valuable than any stories they choose to share. I managed to keep Karen's secret — in part because I still do not know what she was doing in front of that mirror — and she found a respect (admiration?) for a 13-year-old boy she didn't know was possible. I smile when I remember Karen today. Wonder if she remembers me.

14

I saw my grandmother Johnson cry twice. The first time was at Granddaddy's funeral. But everyone was crying there. Gran just seemed to be hurting the way we all did.

The second time I saw Gran cry was the last Monday in July, that last summer when I can remember *not* remembering. She was sitting by herself on the couch in the den. In the very spot I reserved for *Three's Company* reruns. Didn't know it at the time, but it would be a long time before Jack Tripper made me laugh again.

She was still in her robe, the light-blue fabric a contrast to heartbreak. I connect the two now as though Gran planned her outfit. And she had a box of tissues on the sofa's armrest. These were pink. She had one in her hand, bundled up for dabbing the tears on her cheeks. No sign of Libby; still sound asleep in the rear bedroom.

I paused in the doorway, wondering if staying in the hall might be a good decision for today. I guess this was the day I learned what the word *ominous* means.

"Good morning, sugar." Gran somehow smiled

at me, though her face muscles didn't want to. And her eyes weren't smiling.

"What's wrong, Gran?" A couple of steps forward. Gran held out her right hand, and I took it in my left.

"Trey, something awful has happened. Sit down next to your grandmother."

I let go of Gran's hand and did as asked. She now took my right hand in her left, but only after switching that tissue ball to her right.

Again, "What's wrong, Gran?"

"Trey, Devon didn't take his medicine over the weekend."

Devon was a diabetic. I knew this, but paid it as much attention as I did the fact that Larry Blackwell was a Baptist. He took medicine that balanced his blood-sugar level. Insulin. He took shots. Once showed me how he had to pinch the skin in his abdomen, the area where he'd insert the needle. By himself. I would have had a hard time merely pinching myself, but giving myself a shot? Devon was the closest thing to a grown-up I ever saw in a 13-year-old.

"Did he run out?" All I could think of was that Devon didn't have any medicine left. Or maybe he was out of syringes. There had to be something amiss. *He didn't take his medicine?*

"No, Trey. He just didn't take his medicine over the weekend. Mr. and Mrs. McGee were away Saturday night. They found him in shock yesterday." Again, Devon was mature beyond the scope of a junior-high mind. So much so that his parents left him home — the master of the house — if they needed to be away, even overnight.

"What do you mean, they found him in shock? Gran, is Devon okay?"

"He went into insulin shock, Trey. It's called hypoglycemia. His blood-sugar level dropped to a dangerous level."

Now I was scared. And my heart was racing. No spit in my mouth. And Gran's hand felt really cold, as tightly as it held mine.

"Gran, is Devon okay? Where is he?"

"Oh, Trey. I love you so much. And I'm hurting so much, right now. Devon's in heaven, sugar. He died at Cleveland Baptist yesterday. His parents took him to the hospital as fast as they could. But his little body just couldn't hold on."

There are moments in life we want to hang on to forever. And there are moments we'd like to erase the moment they occur. If we're lucky, the two balance each other over the course of time. I needed to erase this moment, tear it to pieces. Go back to bed, get up, and find Gran cooking bacon in the kitchen, a cigarette in her mouth.

"Devon is dead?"

Gran just nodded, barely. I felt a swelling in my throat, as though invisible hands were choking me. As though one dead 13-year-old boy in Cleveland, Tennessee, this week wasn't enough.

Gran let go of my hand and wrapped her left arm around me, pulling me to her side. She was a great hugger. This is the only one I remember that hurt.

"I didn't get to say goodbye."

A selfish thought. Instead of breaking down, saying a prayer for Devon's family, or even asking more questions, my first reaction was about something I missed. Something — in my view — taken away from me. Whether or not it was God (or a god) that did the taking away . . . didn't matter. I didn't get to say goodbye to my friend.

"No one got to say goodbye to Devon, Trey." Gran's voice was trembling now, along with her hands. Her left squeezed my left shoulder and released. Squeezed, and released.

"I don't know how to make this not hurt," she said. "And I don't know why God takes children before their time." In Gran's eyes, God definitely did the taking.

"But we need to view this as Devon's time,

however painful it is to us today. However painful it will be the rest of our lives."

I couldn't talk. My throat was constricting, my tongue felt like sandpaper.

"I want you to know something important, Trey. Something that will help you. Devon knew you loved him."

I looked up at Gran now. Her eyes were wet, the tears yet to fall.

"Boys don't tell each other about love. But I know you loved Devon . . . that you still do. And I know he loved you, Trey. And that *he knew you loved him.*"

Years later, my mom told me that Gran's only question after Granddaddy died was, "Did he know how much I loved him?" It's a question a person asks himself (or herself) when an answer can no longer be provided. Maybe the perfect definition of tragedy. On the most terrible morning of my first 14 years, Gran was making sure I didn't ask the question as much as she did.

I stood up, Gran gently releasing my shoulder. I walked to the sliding glass door, opened it, and stepped out onto Gran's patio. Sat down on the steps that led down to my baseball field. Couldn't imagine even putting on my glove now.

It felt humid, damp even. Long morning

shadows stretched across the back yard. There was no breeze. The chirping of birds — mockingbirds? robins? — gave the yard its summer soundtrack. I could even hear a cricket making its music from somewhere in our neighbor's monkey grass on the other side of the chain-link fence. It felt . . . normal. My throat's tension finally began to release, and the tears came.

I remembered Granddaddy's death, remembered his funeral. Before that, I remembered the shock of learning Elvis Presley had died suddenly in my dad's hometown of Memphis. (Rock stars died? *Elvis died?*) But the shock of a celebrity's death combined with the permanence of Granddaddy's passing somehow didn't prepare me for the heavy emptiness of my friend's death at age 13. Thirteen! I didn't know what young was; to me, anyone over the age of 20 lived in a different world, where comic books and curiosity were forbidden. But I knew 13 was young . . . because it was my age. (Again, a selfish thought.)

I tried to imagine what Devon was thinking then. Was he sitting atop some cloud high above me, already getting used to life with wings on his back, a halo hovering over his black curls? Maybe he was in line at the pearly gates. Lots of people die every day, all over the world. Did Devon stand out, so small, so young? Did you get to cut to the front of the line if you were taken suddenly, without a full life for St. Peter to evaluate? Devon wasn't patient. He wouldn't like any line in heaven, no matter the rules or format.

But what if Devon couldn't think at all anymore? What if it was just . . . nothing. Nothingness. As I tried to breathe normally, tried to compose my thoughts around that cricket's tune, this was the thought that tortured me. The assault of nothingness. However active or inactive we might be, however young or old, black or white, wherever we call home, the central joy of living was the ability to think. To consider. To wonder. To gaze at a patio wall and see a strike zone. To call an old oak tree a third baseman. What if death took this away completely? The assault of nothingness horrified me, and still does.

"NOOOOOOOOOOOOOOOOO!!!"

Libby screamed from inside the house. She had just heard about Devon. Surely Gran was now holding her tight, probably rocking my 8-year-old sister as though she were seven years younger.

I was envious of Libby. Not for being rocked by Gran. But for being able to scream like that. Why couldn't I scream? I wanted to scream. Desperately. I wanted the world to hear my scream and I wanted Devon — even if trapped in nothingness — to hear my scream. But for now, Libby's wail would have to do.

I rubbed the back of my hands against my cheeks, then down the side of my pajama pants. (The logos of every NFL team. How did that image sneak into this nightmare?) I got up and walked back inside. Gran was where I left her, on the couch, rocking Libby in her arms just as I had pictured.

My little sister then did something I'll never forget. It was something stronger than I would have imagined her capable of. But something that told me a lot about who she was, and who she is today.

Libby got up from Gran's lap and ran to hug me. My sister and I grew up a lot with that hug. Somehow, it seemed to start my recovery. Devon was gone, and his absence was painfully permanent. But so was the bond I had with Libby.

The next four days were the longest, loneliest, quietest summer days I can remember. Gran got out one of her 1,000-piece crossword puzzles — a mountain stream next to a cabin — to help pass the long hours. I'd normally join her in searching for shades that match. But focus had left me.

Backyard baseball was therapeutic, or should have been. Instead of Tommy Herr as my second-baseman — the small tree to the left of my "pitcher's mound" — I put Devon in the lineup. If I could play shortstop for Cleveland's version of the St. Louis

Cardinals, Devon could sure as hell play second. This distraction worked a little better than the jigsaw puzzle.

Gran's smoking picked up. She was what I'd call a semi-private society smoker. She didn't smoke when playing with Libby or me. Didn't smoke in public unless offered a light by another smoker. But in the days after Devon's death, I found her occasionally sitting at the kitchen table, puffing on a Camel. She often smoked when washing the dishes. (Despite having a dishwasher, Gran liked to do small loads by hand.) And she smoked when cooking a meal.

She kept a box of Diamond kitchen matches right next to the kitchen sink, between the dishwashing liquid and the toaster. My mom and dad — both smokers — kept little matchbooks nearby, or maybe a lighter. But Gran had this box where you'd slide out a compartment packed with sturdy, wooden matches. "Strike On Box" was written on the top of the container. She'd remove a match and, quickly as snapping her fingers, would slam it against the rough side of that box. It was an ugly habit, but Gran lit a match like a pro.

On Tuesday, Gran took me to Etowah, to buy me a suit at Caldwell's. A suit for Devon's funeral, which would be on Friday at Cleveland Methodist. The store manager — Eli, was his name — gave me his full attention, as though I were an attorney, to be dressed for the trial of the century. The suit was black, with pinstripes. Heavy attire for a 13-year-old boy. I was already 5'9", though, so it came off the rack in the men's section.

The shoes were black, shiny, without strings. Just slid on my feet, so accustomed to sneakers. Why on earth should a boy be comfortable, though, in attending the funeral of his friend? This was an important process, I knew, and Gran steered me through it with her typical compassion. She even smiled when I came out of the dressing room with the outfit — minus a tie — complete.

"I've never seen such a handsome young man," she said. "We'll need to send a picture to your mom and dad."

When I looked at myself in the mirror, the "grown-up me" stared back, and he wasn't smiling. My hair flared out over my ears, right where my Cardinal cap pressed them east and west when it wanted to fall south. (Morning baseball after my shower tended to shape my drying hair for the rest of the day.) Maybe it was my hair that did it, but I looked like a boy from the neck up . . . and an accountant below my shoulders. Devon would have laughed so hard if he had seen me in that mirror. Did he?

"Maybe I should change back, Gran. I know Libby needs to find a dress." My sister was on the other side of the store, in the hands of an outfitter in the ladies department.

"That's fine," said Gran. "What do you think of this tie?" The cravat (as Auntie would call it) had dark red — maroon — stripes, slanted against black. A touch of color.

"It's fine," I conceded. "Thanks, Gran."

Why do we wait until someone is dead to dress up in their honor? This thought haunted me on the drive home, my new suit dangling from the hook above the rear, passenger-side window.

Gran had Slim Whitman crooning on her eight-track player. ("Rose Marie" was her favorite, but "Tomorrow Never Comes" tends to stick out in my memory.) Staring out the window, I kept seeing things I knew Devon wouldn't. Including that suit. Hard to process.

15

On Thursday, the day before the funeral, I ventured out on my bike for the first time since learning of Devon's death. Part of the healing, I'd later recognize, was doing what I'd normally do. And normally, I'd be riding around Gran's neighborhood with my best friend. Without Devon, the closest I could approximate this behavior was to be on my bike, sweating through my blue jeans and under my Cardinal hat, riding somewhere.

I rode by Wendy's house, but didn't know how I would talk to her, or if we'd even have words to exchange in Devon's absence. The basketball hoop in her driveway just stood there, as lonely as I felt. Jerry's car — a green Pinto — was in the driveway. Which made the hoop look even lonelier.

Larry Blackwell lived on the other side of the hill that served as a divide between the middle class (like Gran and the Nickersons) and the wealthy Chattanooga commuters (like Larry's dad). Riding along Martindale Avenue, up and over this hill, you saw homes go from modest three-bedrooms (like Gran's) to enormous almost-mansions, often with three-car garages that seemed to say *one-car-per-adult isn't enough for our lifestyle.* The Blackwells had a three-car garage.

I hadn't heard from Larry all week, which was odd. His silence told me as much about the impact of our friend's passing as any tears I witnessed. Larry and Devon were friendly rivals, at best. Devon's love for his orange bike and Larry's shunning of such a transportation booster made for a nice metaphor between personalities as divergent as their skin colors. But Larry had clearly met up with something beyond his capacity to reduce with sarcasm or insults. Death silences so much more than the deceased.

I knocked on Larry's door, and his mom answered. "Well hi, Trey." Mrs. Blackwell had a kind smile, however much makeup she used to enhance it. Her hair was as black as Larry's, which made it easy to hide the dye she used as gray began to appear. "Let me get Larry. He's upstairs."

For the first time since I'd known Larry Blackwell — this was our third summer together — I wondered if I was imposing. If I didn't know what I'd say to Wendy, what exactly was I going to say to Larry?

"Hey, Trey." Larry was wearing, quite possibly, the ugliest shirt I ever saw (to this day). Broad horizontal stripes, green and brown alternating. If

Charlie Brown had crossed over to the dark side, he would have worn this shirt. I actually started laughing, and for the first time since Monday.

"What's so funny?" Larry hadn't a clue how dramatically ill his fashion sense was, and he wasn't going to share any humor I might illuminate from his earth-tones-gone-bad shirt of choice.

"Nothing. Just remembered something on *Three's Company* today." Normally, any reference to our favorite sitcom would trigger a comment from Larry about Suzanne Somers' breasts (and Larry's theory that her contract stipulated that she was not allowed to wear a bra on the set of the show). But not today.

"It really sucks. You know, about Devon." For Larry Blackwell, this constituted hysterics.

"Yeah. Sucks. Are you going to the funeral tomorrow?"

"I don't know," he said. "Pretty depressing. You know, he was tough. For such a little guy." Larry wasn't that much taller than Devon. Both "little guys" when standing next to me.

"I guess it was his toughness that killed him," said Larry. "He didn't like those shots." For Larry Blackwell, this constituted a eulogy.

Just inside Larry's house, you could feel the late July heat trespassing through the Blackwells' screen door.

Mixing with the air conditioning, it challenged your body to decide whether to be cool or warm. Much like 13-year-olds anticipating a mid-summer funeral had to decide whether it was time to play or cry.

"I'm playing Atari," said Larry. "Wanna play?"

Larry didn't like bikes, strangely enough. And I didn't like video games . . . strangely enough, I supposed. Fending off space invaders or steering Pac Man along a maze of munchies just didn't inspire me. Maybe too many baseball statistics in my brain.

"I don't think so. Just wanted to see what you were doing, and if you're going to the funeral." Don't know why I brought it up a second time.

"Let's go bug Arline sometime. She loves it, you know." It's the first time I'd thought of Arline since Monday. I was surprised that her name comforted me.

"Yeah, we should. Okay . . . I'll see ya later."

The screen door clapped shut behind me, and the temperature was no longer ambiguous. Steaming hot. As I got back on my bike, I wondered how (or if) Devon could feel this heat. *Do the dead pay attention to weather?* And if he couldn't feel the heat that was currently opening my pores, I thought, how unfair. But that was just it, right? Feeling the heat — or air conditioning, or rain, or wind — confirmed we were

133

alive. And Devon was dead. Once again, the permanence of it all swallowed me whole.

* * *

The suit was okay. I actually liked the way it looked on me, staring at myself in Gran's full-length mirror. (The one Karen Dunham made unforgettable.) If you want to add five years — at least — to a boy's age, just put him in a suit.

My neck was protesting, though. And when you think about it, that's where the discomfort of a men's suit begins and ends: the neck. Unbutton that collar, loosen that tie, and you may as well be in slacks and a long-sleeved t-shirt. But with that Caldwell's cravat seeming to squeeze my throat shut, there would be no comfort today. Which was as it should be.

My churchgoing days could be counted on one hand. I had a vague recollection of a Christmas pageant in Memphis, one my paternal grandmother took us to before I was old enough to even consider the faith component. When the subject of worship came up at our house — and it was seldom — Dad liked to say, "God cares just as much how you act from Monday to Saturday as He does where you're sitting on Sunday morning."

He and my mom had had their share of Sunday school as children. As Libby and I grew up, they seemed more interested in us paying attention to the

newspaper on Sunday mornings, or even the longwinded commentary from
the news-makers on television. Do right by God from Monday to Saturday, and we seemed to have our Sundays to ourselves.

With Devon's funeral on a Friday, it felt less like an invasion of Cleveland Methodist. More like a visit to a place big enough — with the necessary steeple, and a cross above the front doors — to accommodate Devon's family and friends. Scheduled for 11 o'clock in the morning, it was late enough not to feel urgent, and under sunshine that seemed to lessen the gravity of the event.

Cleveland Methodist was on the east side of Cleveland, "the outskirts of town" as Gran described it. You had to drive through Cleveland's retail strip — past the Arby's, Roses (Gran's favorite department store), the Twin Cinema, and three blocks of car dealerships — to reach "the outskirts."

The church was indeed massive, set back from its two-lane street by an enormous gravel parking lot. (I later wondered about that gravel. Dad told me there was a lot of money in prayer. If that was the case, why couldn't Cleveland Methodist pave its parking lot?)

A large field lay to the left of the church, the grass left to grow and bend with the breeze, whether it blew on Sunday or any other day of the week. Behind the church, I discovered that Friday, was a basketball hoop.

A single post with a backboard, rim, and chain net. The lot that spilled behind the church — where Gran was forced to park — was no more paved than in the front, but under the hoop the rocks had been kicked, spread, and shoved by enough sneakers that a patch of ground clean and flat enough to dribble a basketball presented a secular touch to a place that seemed far too heavy for a 13-year-old boy.

"Libby, you hold Gran's hand. Lots of cars."

As we got out of Gran's tan Buick, I realized her four-door sedan wasn't nearly as big as I liked to imagine. (Mom drove a Datsun back home, Dad a cool but creaky old Triumph.) The parking lot — front and back — was filled with sedans just as big as Gran's. More Buicks, Oldsmobiles, even a few Cadillacs. Family cars, I suppose. Funeral cars, maybe.

"My shoes are already dirty, Gran."

Libby had shiny black shoes, the kind that buckle on top. And the gravel was turning them more gray with every step she took.

"Don't worry, darlin'," said Gran. "Shoes can get dirty. Let's keep that beautiful dress clean."

The dress was white, with sky-blue stripes that ran vertically. Libby was beautiful. I wasn't sure if Devon would recognize her.

"Good mornin', Cooper."

As we turned around the front of the church, we found Flossie Hilgarten standing near the top of the steps that ran the length of the building.

"Why, good morning, Flossie." Gran smiled, let go of Libby's hand for a moment, and squeezed Flossie in a hug. They looked pretty, each in her black dress, Flossie's hair up, her lipstick a brownish red that seemed to be as thick as paint. (Flossie's bra was completely hidden, but I knew what color it was. Damn the visual imagery.)

"I've never seen such a handsome young man, or as lovely a little lady."

The fact that Flossie saw both Libby and me all summer made her comment an obvious stretch, but it was loving, like the person who said it. Libby hugged her.

With cars still pulling into the lot — around to the back now, where we'd parked — Gran, Flossie, my sister, and I walked into the church.

There's no way to prepare for seeing a dead body the first time. Just hope that when you do, it was like my experience: in a church, the body in a suit (or dress), comfortably at rest in a coffin.

The blast of air conditioning when we entered the sanctuary was merely the first chill of the day. The size of the building was somehow reduced by the number of people gradually filling each pew.

I found myself taking baby-steps as we moved inside, staring forward, down the center aisle. Gran had warned me about an open casket, but fear tends to trump preparation. And I was scared of what I'd see in that casket.

From the back of the church, I couldn't even see the casket, let alone Devon. A line that formed on the right side of the sanctuary — under tall windows that arched to a point at their tops — snaked along the side of the pews, then in front, past Devon's casket. Past Devon's body.

Gran put her arm around my back and gently tugged on my left shoulder, toward the back of a line I never wanted to enter. Never wanted to reach the front of this line. Libby held Gran's right hand, her eyes wide. She was probably afraid, too.

It was the largest indoor gathering I'd ever seen in Cleveland. And the familiar faces made me feel less like the outsider I tended to consider myself in the summer months.

There were at least five pews on the front, right side filled with black people. Devon's family. He was an only child, but three of his grandparents were alive, and he had aunts, uncles, cousins. Some of the kids among his family were younger than me. Younger than Devon was when he died.

Was that comforting or tragic?

Then there were Devon's classmates. You could tell by glancing from pew to pew, across the center aisle, to the back of the church as people continued to enter. Boys and girls around 13 years old, each with at least one parent, but otherwise alone, save for a sibling or two. That's what made it strange. In any other setting, 13-year-olds gravitate to one another. Social circles are born in junior high. But not at a funeral.

There was Larry with his parents, near the back on the left side of the aisle. His hair was actually slicked back, combed like his father did every day on his way to legal battles in Chattanooga.

There was Arline, a few rows in front of the Blackwells. Her dress was dark green. She stared forward, just like her mom. She was pretty. It helped to see her.

There was the Dunham family, on the right side of the aisle, not too far behind Devon's family. All I could see was the back of Karen's head, her hair as shiny as always. I could picture much more.

Then I saw Geraldine walk in. The ice cream lady. And she made me start to cry. She wore a black dress, with two large, yellow butterflies traced in what looked like glitter beneath her shoulders. She also wore a large, black hat, the kind that allowed light through the tiny holes, but not enough to burn on a summer day. Geraldine sat down in the very back row, all the way to the left side of the church. She apparently wasn't interested in this line of misery.

Geraldine brought tears to my eyes because — until that moment — my association with her was entirely smiles and laughter. The person who brings ice cream to children ranks right up there with circus ringmaster or baseball coach. He — or she — packages joy.

To see Geraldine dressed up, by herself (did she drive her truck to the church?), and as sad as the rest of us was too heavy for my attempts at stoic composure. I was glad she didn't see me.

We reached the point in the line where we turned to walk by Devon's casket. I didn't have the courage to turn and look at his family as I walked by. If Geraldine had my cheeks wet, what would seeing Devon's parents do to me?

And there he was. Sleeping. He had to be sleeping. I'd spent the night with Devon on a few occasions — usually at Gran's house — and I'd never seen him look more peaceful. His head rested on a satin pillow, slightly raised, as if he needed to see something on his chest. He wore a tan suit, with a dark brown tie that contrasted against his white shirt in a way Devon would have considered stylish.

Devon insisted that black people should wear light suits and white people should wear dark suits. A rule he felt was horribly violated by John Travolta in *Saturday Night Fever*. He was convinced disco died because a white man wore a white suit.

The lid to the casket was divided, Devon's legs covered by one section. And I found myself wondering what kind of shoes he was wearing. Devon's dad once told him that the key to happiness was a comfortable bed and comfortable shoes. I wondered if Devon would be buried in comfortable shoes. A silly notion, I suppose.

Gran squeezed my shoulder tightly as we walked by (we never stopped). Libby stared curiously, her eyes barely high enough to see inside the casket. It wasn't until we were beyond the casket and turning up the left side of the church to find our seats that I noticed the soft hymns playing on the sound system.

Funny how our senses close down at times, deferring to one another. As my eyes prepared for a sight beyond their capability of processing, my ears

141

apparently took a breather. The sound of those hymns was comforting, and made me feel closer to normal.

Gran steered us down a row midway between the front and back of the sanctuary. Close enough to see Devon's family across the aisle. But not so close to feel the squeeze of fear and sorrow that gripped us when we walked by Devon's sleeping form.

Then I saw Wendy. I'd missed her as we were walking back, but there she was, three rows in front of where we were now sitting. She was at the very end of the pew, next to her brother Jerry, her parents to Jerry's right. Her dress was dark purple, her blond hair falling toward her shoulder blades. I could see a single barrette holding up the hair that would have otherwise covered her right cheek.

And I could see Wendy's shoulders trembling.

I'm not really sure how to define bravery. Perhaps it's doing something you don't want to do, but know you have to do, however uncomfortable it may be. Seeing Wendy's shoulders shake led me to the single bravest act of my childhood. And it changed forever my last summer in Cleveland.

"Gran, there's Wendy. I'm gonna go sit next to her."

Gran smiled at me and patted my right knee gently. "You go ahead."

I shuffled along our row to the left side of the church, almost stumbling over the foot of a large, bearded man who seemed irritated, as though my passing cost him a scene in a movie.

"Pardon me. Sorry. Need to see someone."

Once in the aisle — again under those arched windows that today seemed to make the church excessively bright — my palms got sweaty. Wendy was at the end of her row, just to the left of her brother, with her parents to Jerry's right. There was room on Wendy's pew, though, for at least two more people. I walked up to the row and, without turning really, slid into the space to Wendy's left. Heart racing.

"Hey."

She looked at me, both cheeks glistening from tears she hadn't wiped. I noticed she had a bundled tissue in her right hand. Why hadn't she wiped the tears?

"Hi, Trey."

I've never seen someone so sad look so beautiful. I turned forward to keep myself from staring at her. If she didn't notice, someone else would.

"It doesn't seem real," I said. It really didn't. Here I was at my friend's funeral, and I was precisely where I *wanted* to be at that moment.

"Seems *too* real." Wendy corrected me. It was all too real.

She slid slightly to the left — closer to me — and rested her head on my right shoulder, surely dampening my new suit with her tears. But her shoulders weren't shaking anymore. Clichés are born for a reason, and I've never read or heard the words *a shoulder to cry on* the same way since Devon's funeral. I glanced slightly down; could see the top of Wendy's head. And my heart actually slowed. Calmed down. This felt right.

The music was softened gradually until silence filled the sanctuary. Almost every head turned toward the back of the church. (Why is a church's entrance called "the back"?) Rev. Avery Jameson had entered the building.

Years later, I'd see pictures of Rufus Thomas, the legendary entertainer from Memphis, and I was convinced he'd used a different name during summers in east Tennessee. Rev. Jameson looked that much like Rufus Thomas. Bald, a gray beard, eyes that seemed as though they'd leap from his skull. He wore a black suit with thick, gray stripes. Supposed to "thin" a man, Gran later explained.

Rev. Jameson was one of the first men I saw who had what's called presence. Without saying a word, you knew he was in the room. His personality — his *being* — was quite the opposite of "thinning."

Rev. Jameson walked slowly up the center aisle, never taking his gaze off of Devon. He had to know every person in every pew was staring at him, but he kept those bulging eyes forward, on the reason we were all here.

When he got near the front, he turned and nodded to Devon's extended family. Paused. He then walked along the front row, shaking the hands of Mr. McGee and hugging Mrs. McGee. Now it was Mrs. McGee's shoulders I could see trembling.

As Rev. Jameson walked up the three stairs to the platform where he'd deliver Devon's eulogy, Wendy again rested her head on my right shoulder. I noticed two things when she did. Her tan calves — above the black sandals she wore — were enough to make my heart race again.

I'd seen Wendy's bare legs on plenty of occasions, but never under a dress as pretty as the one she wore today.

I also noticed that Wendy's wrists were bruised. Both of them. Why?

* * *

"Every time I finish The Book, I'm disappointed." Rev. Jameson tipped his chin upward as he began, but gazed down at us. He wasn't so much frowning as clenching his jaw.

145

"You know The Book I'm talking about, friends. The only Book that teaches, that preaches . . . that *reaches* us. The Book that reaches every living soul. Yes indeed, every time I finish The Book, I'm disappointed."

I didn't know quite where the pastor was going with this. A man of the cloth disappointed with the Bible?

"Why does the Book disappoint me? You gotta be wonderin' . . . why is Rev. Jameson disappointed in the holy word? What's that old man sayin'?"

I was wondering.

"Every time I finish The Book, I'm disappointed . . . because it's too short. It's not enough for me, not enough for my heart to be filled entirely, for my soul to swell to its maximum size! The Book is my most precious possession, friends. And . . . it's . . . too . . . short. Just like Devon McGee's life."

Connection made. Wendy and I glanced at each other, her eyes welling with more tears.

"We can be selfish as we spend our days in this life," Rev. Jameson continued. "We want all we can get, and all the time. The fanciest homes, the nicest cars, the high-paying jobs. But most of all, we want those closest to us to be near, to enrich us — to *reach us* just like The Book — as often as they can."

After a dramatic pause, he continued, "And

Devon reached us all. Needless to say, he was the McGee family's most precious possession. And his life was much, much too short."

I turned back to look at Gran and Libby. My grandmother's head was tilted slightly to the right, her brow furrowed. She looked midway between heartbroken and angry . . . which is probably precisely where she was. As for my sister, she was listening, but distracted. Looking up at the vaulted ceiling, out the arched windows into the sunshine (still out of place, in my view, for this setting).

Beyond my family, all the way to the back, I caught a glimpse of Geraldine again. Heard "The Saints Go Marching In" for a moment, but just a moment. There was no anger in Geraldine's face. Only sorrow.

"As disappointed as we may be today," continued Rev. Jameson, "as sad as we are at the passing of young Devon, we need to consider ourselves — once again — blessed. That's right, friends. We are blessed. For we knew Devon McGee. We let Devon McGee enter our hearts. We let Devon McGee help shape our spirit, friends!

"Too often, we old folks act as though we're shaping the lives of those who follow us, the children who gaze up into our eyes with wonderment and curiosity. We aim to steer them in the right direction, to lead by example — and by the word of the Book.

"But friends, sometimes it's the other way around. Sometimes the young folks among us — and there are lots of you in this building today — do the leading, and the steering.

"Devon McGee led us, you see. He led us to a place of love and friendship, the most precious place we'll ever know outside heaven. He may not have had much time in this world. But his spirit took advantage of the time he did have. His *soul* took advantage of every minute he had!"

Wendy would jump slightly when Rev. Jameson raised his voice. Couldn't tell if it was merely the volume, or a sense of threat. Her tissue remained clenched in her right hand, her cheeks still damp.

Devon's mom, in the front row, had her head bowed, the way you'd bow in prayer. But I think it was because she couldn't look at her son's body in that coffin, only a few feet in front of her. Mr. McGee, to her right, had his head straight up, his broad shoulders erect. A picture of strength I'll never forget.

"The lesson we must learn from Devon, friends, is to take advantage of every minute we have. How old are you today? Seventy? Forty? Twenty-five . . . in the prime of your life? I know some of you are 13."

Yep, 13. Never felt older.

"Whatever your age may be . . . ." Rev. Jameson paused and scanned the gathering, right to left. Seemed as though he was looking at me, then Wendy, as he slowly turned his head. "Take advantage of every minute. Lead us to a place of love and friendship, just as Devon McGee did. Better yet, lead *others* to that place of love and friendship . . . *and remind them that Devon McGee showed you the way.*"

I remembered reading Mark Twain's *Tom Sawyer*, and getting a kick out of Tom attending his own funeral. For some reason, that memory snuck into my head as I fought for a sense of normalcy. One of my best friends was dead, I was quite possibly falling in love with the girl sitting to my right (never more beautiful as she suffered this moment with me), my parents were two thousand miles away, and Tom Sawyer entered my brain. What a kick Devon would have gotten if he could be here (in a pew, or maybe hiding in a closet) today.

"There will be a private burial at North Meadow," said Rev. Jameson. "At four o'clock this afternoon, Mr. and Mrs. Robert Tillman will host a gathering at their lovely home." The Tillmans were among Devon's aunts and uncles. They lived on a small lake, halfway to Chattanooga. "You'll be given directions to the Tillman home as you leave the building."

From behind Rev. Jameson, through a door I didn't even see until it opened, came a small choir of six women (all of them black, all of them in red gowns). After taking position behind Devon's casket, they began singing "Amazing Grace."

The McGee family rose to their feet and slowly walked down the center aisle and out of the church.

That was it. My first funeral. When we got up to leave, Wendy squeezed my right hand with her left. She didn't hold it; we had different directions to go. But she squeezed my hand. May as well have reached inside my chest and squeezed my heart directly. My first funeral and, somehow, the only one that today brings a smile. Hard to explain.

16

"Are you sure we're supposed to go? This is for kids?"

I was sitting at Gran's table, still in my coat and tie, nibbling on one of her grilled-cheese sandwiches. (They were the best grilled-cheese sandwiches ever cooked. Gran snuck some vinaigrette dressing between the cheese and bread. I've tried to duplicate the recipe. Can't.) Libby was across the table. She insisted on her sandwich being cut into two triangles. Gran didn't need to be asked.

"This isn't for kids or adults, Trey," said Gran from the sink, where she was wiping down the frying pan. "It's for Devon's friends, and friends of the McGee family. You're certainly one."

"Will they have cake at this party?" asked Libby. The funeral may as well have been twelve months ago.

"I wouldn't count on it, sugar," said Gran, smiling. "But if they do, we'll make sure you get a slice."

"It's not a party. Don't act like it is." Rarely did I scold my little sister, but I had no interest in stretching this miserable day another minute, let alone long enough to visit the Tillman house.

"Easy, Trey. Libby knows this isn't a celebration." Gran had a way of elevating the spirit of the accosted without doing so directly.

"They want people to feel better, don't they?" Another inquiry from the all-seeing 8-year-old. "Well, cake makes people feel better."

* * *

There was no Slim Whitman played on the drive to Ooltewah. No music at all. The tiny town was almost precisely halfway between Cleveland and Chattanooga. Didn't take more than thirty minutes to get there. Why does time rush when we're heading toward something we dread?

"How long are we going to stay?" I was prepared to start a countdown if I could find a clock. And judging by the size of the Tillman home — set back from the highway almost a half-mile — there would be plenty of clocks at this gathering.

"We're staying long enough to pay our respects, darlin'. As long as that takes."

"What do I say? Will Larry be here?"

"He may be. You just be sure to find Devon's parents. Better yet, we'll find them together."

Cars were parked one behind the other, lining each side of the Tillmans' gargantuan driveway. Two horses grazed beyond a rail fence to the right of the driveway. Mr. Tillman was a stockbroker. He made money by making money for other people. At least that's the way Gran described him. Enough money to own two horses and pave a half-mile driveway.

"Can we ride the horses?" Again, Libby.

"Not today, honey."

"What are their names?"

"We'll ask Mr. and Mrs. Tillman. That's a good question."

Gran grabbed Libby's hand. Mine dangled uselessly at my side. Gran said a gentleman doesn't walk with his hands in his pockets. I felt useless, and somehow foreign, approaching the oversized red door of the Tillman home. Gran rang the doorbell. A housekeeper — dressed in a tan smock — opened the door immediately. (This was a lesson in itself. A black housekeeper employed by a black family. Not an arrangement I would have imagined before today.)

"Good afternoon," she said. "Please come inside." How do people smile when gathering to honor the dead? But they do. They smile.

"I'm Cooper Johnson, from Cleveland. These are my grandchildren, Libby and Trey."

"So nice to meet you. I'm Doris."

The house was packed. Hallways, too. I was tall for my age, but not tall enough to see over the shoulder-to-shoulder mass of humanity gathered here to, somehow, comfort each other. But I could see enough in five minutes of surveying to tell there weren't any other kids here, at least none I recognized. No Larry. No Wendy. (I was hoping to find her.) I would have settled for Arline. Would have loved to see Geraldine, an honorary kid. Just as I suspected, this was going to be miserable. Grow up, Trey. Fast.

Gran led us into the largest room we'd seen yet. The ceiling must have been twenty feet high. An enormous couch in the shape of an "L" centered the room, a large console television against one wall. Behind the couch, along a half-wall that opened into the kitchen was a long counter. And on that counter were framed pictures of Devon. Must have been thirty of them, some tiny, some clearly taken from the walls of various family members.

Smiling. Devon smiling at me from one picture after another. There he was as a baby, that smile the same I'd seen just a week ago. (Remember, smiles don't age.) It's a fact of life: black babies are cuter than white babies. They just look healthier, more vibrant. And the puff of curls on Devon's infant head. I actually grinned, considering how Devon would have reacted if I called him cute.

A hand touched the side of my right arm from

behind. It was Mrs. McGee. I wasn't prepared. My throat tightened, and I felt the tears welling as I looked into her face for the first time since my friend died. Since her son died. And she was smiling. How is that possible?

Without saying a word, she opened her arms and pulled me into one of the most important hugs of my life. "I'm so glad you're here, Trey. Devon loved you so much. Summer was his favorite time of year."

Devon loved me? He wouldn't have admitted to even liking me, not verbally. I held Mrs. McGee tightly, even rested my head on her shoulder. My throat was too tight for me to talk.

"I've got something for you, Trey." Mrs. McGee had an envelope in her left hand, the one that had just held me, patted my back as we were hugging.

"I found this in Devon's desk. It had to be for you."

My name was written on the envelope in script. Mrs. McGee's writing, I assumed. The envelope wasn't sealed, so it opened easily. Inside was a 3-D baseball card of Ted Simmons. The Cardinal catcher. One of my first heroes.

The 3-D cards were a gimmick of Kellogg's cereal. Their version of the Cracker Jack surprise, an attempt to sell a few more boxes of cereal to eager card collectors willing to shovel Frosted Flakes down their throats to complete a 30-card collection. The 3-D effect was gained through ribbed plastic coating, but the coating made the cards curl in a way no baseball card should. The series had been discontinued two or three years before Devon's death. Simmons had been playing for the Milwaukee Brewers the last two seasons. Mrs. McGee was right.

If this gaudy baseball card of Ted Simmons was in Devon's desk, it had to be for me. He'd just forgotten to give it to me. Probably fell out of a cereal box in the dead of winter, the middle of a school year. Devon — seeing a Cardinal posing with a bat over his shoulder — had held the prize for me. It was touching. Which almost made me grin again.

"He was my best friend," I said, staring at the 3-D Simmons. (And yes, Simmons stared back.)

"Devon, I mean." I looked up at Mrs. McGee, who was smiling. "Devon was my best friend. Not Ted Simmons, this guy." I showed Mrs. McGee the face of the card, as though she hadn't seen it already.

"I know what you mean, Trey." She grabbed my right arm with her left hand, more firmly than I expected.

"He's still your best friend, Trey. You're going to miss him terribly, as I do. As we all do. But he's still your best friend. Don't forget that. And hang on to that card."

"I will, Mrs. McGee. Thank you." The lump in my throat was gone. I actually felt more normal than I had all day. I wasn't sure if it was the brief conversation with Mrs. McGee (if she could carry on, I sure as hell could) or the Ted Simmons card. But I felt almost inspired.

I put the card back inside the envelope, and placed the envelope inside my jacket. It fit perfectly in that slot where mobsters were always hiding envelopes stuffed with cash. Made me feel like the 3-D gift from my dead friend was loot. Tucked safely inside my suit, I'd make it home with the package. No problem.

Across the room, sitting on the end of the Tillmans' extravagant couch was Gran. And next to her . . . Flossie. I hadn't seen Flossie during my first walk-through. But there she was, dabbing mascara and talking to Gran. Two elderly white ladies in the home of a wealthy black family they wouldn't have known were it not for Devon's sudden death. And talking with each other as though they were negotiating a peace treaty . . . somewhere. Libby sat next to Gran with a tall glass of lemonade in her hands. She was listening to the peace negotiations. We wouldn't be leaving soon.

I casually opened the front door and stepped

outside. There was some lawn furniture — metal, but painted white — to the left of the entrance. I sat down in one of the chairs, content with the solitude and the sound of locusts filling the late afternoon twilight. The sound — did locusts hum? squeal? creak? — got louder as I sat there. The louder it got, the better it felt. Like a good hug.

* * *

Thwap. The sound was the same with every pitch.

Thwap. Ground ball to me at shortstop. I flip to Devon at second, who makes the turn to complete the double play. End of the inning . . . Cardinals coming up.

In the days after Devon's funeral, my games of solo baseball in Gran's backyard continued, only with Devon taking the place of Tommy Herr at second base (that small pear tree).

My game, my rules, my team, and my roster. Hernandez at first, Milligan at short, and two McGees on this Cardinal team: Willie in centerfield, Devon at second base.

Thwap.

The multi-colored rubber ball bounced true, but the ridges, angles, and cracks of the brick wall that formed Gran's patio made for irregular grounders, line drives, and occasional pop-ups.

158

As the Cardinal shortstop, I had to be prepared
for anything. As the Cardinal pitcher, every play
began with my release.

Thwap.

I wore my red Cardinal hat low, just above my
eyebrows, the way I'd seen Bob Gibson wear his hat
in the pictures Dad showed me. (Gran complained
when we sent her family pictures, as she couldn't see
anything but my chin from under the bill of the cap.)
The hat helped me focus by eliminating 25 percent of
my peripheral vision. Just me, the batter, and my two
firmly rooted infielders.

Thwap.

A sharp grounder slightly to my right . . . I field
it cleanly, plant my right foot, and hurl the ball back
at the patio wall — first-baseman Keith Hernandez
now — to force the runner in plenty of time.

"Safe!"

Huh?

It was Arline. She was walking up to the chain-
link fence that served as my field's home-run wall.
Nothing peripheral vision can do for a pitcher when
approached from behind.

"He beat the throw, Trey. It was Tim Raines."
Raines was the base-stealing outfielder for the
Montreal Expos.

"It wasn't Raines, and he was out."

Already sweating through my gray Cardinal T-shirt, I found myself debating a character in my imaginary baseball world. Maturity awaited, patiently.

"You double-pumped the throw," said Arline. "He was safe. Next batter."

"Do you need something?" Aggravation mixed with discomfort. Part of the joy of my solitary baseball outings was being solitary. Actually, that was the primary joy of these games.

Arline placed both her arms atop the chain-link (it was kid-friendly, no barbed rim at the top). Rested her chin on her folded hands, as though settling in for the game. "Why don't you play catch with Wendy?"

The memory of the Fourth of July — and playing catch with Wendy — almost snuck from my brain to my tongue. But I kept it to myself and shifted to curiosity at the question.

"What are you talking about? She's not here."

"It's a short walk to her house. You and Larry go there all the time."

I noticed she didn't include Devon in this broad declaration.

"I'm not going to Wendy's house to play catch with her, Arline. Why don't you?" Again, maturity tapping its foot patiently.

"Well, I saw you sitting with her at Devon's funeral. Seems like you and her are pretty close."

Clarity. This was a matter of envy, somehow. Arline didn't like seeing me with another woman, not even at a friend's funeral.

"I sat with a lot of people at the funeral, Arline." Not true, really.

"Doesn't mean we're any closer than we've ever been." Not true, either.

"You seem pretty close, Trey. Are you gonna take her on a date?"

RUMMMMMMMMMMMMM-BA-BA-BA-BA-BA-BA-BA-BA-BABA!!!!!

Gran's back yard was suddenly filled with the roar of whirling metal, and burning gasoline. Could only mean one thing: Flossie was mowing her yard. Her timing couldn't be better.

From the side of her house blind to Arline and me, Flossie emerged behind her green John Deere lawn mower. Her hair bundled atop her head, oversized sunglasses covering half her face, white shorts . . . and nothing above her waist but a lacy black bra. She smiled and waved at Arline and me. "Mornin' kids!"

The volume of the mower ended any chance that Arline and I would pursue the romantic angle of my relationship with Wendy Nickerson. Needing to practically shout to be heard over the fence, the conversation grew blessedly mundane. And Arline's focus was now in the next yard.

"I can't believe she does that!" It's funny to hear someone shout a whisper. Not an easy thing to pull off.

"She keeps cool," I said, smiling. I tipped my hat back, enough to wipe the sweat from my forehead.

"The whole neighborhood can see her!" Another whisper, shouted.

"Do you think Flossie cares, Arline? Do you think she'd care if an entire baseball stadium saw her?"

She laughed. Even bent over a bit. Arline was pretty when she laughed. And I laughed with her. Tossed the ball back toward the patio, where it rested the remainder of the day.

17

The package arrived on a Thursday afternoon. I remember, because it barely fit in Gran's mailbox, cramming my new issue of *Sports Illustrated* — one with Ray (Boom Boom) Mancini on the cover — to the side. (This was a few months before Mancini beat South Korean Duk Koo Kim to death in the ring.) It was from my parents, my mom's distinctive script spelling out my full, formal name: Mr. Charles Michael Milligan III.

Mom and Dad sent Libby and me care packages periodically, as though we were at a distant summer camp. (I suppose we were.) Homemade brownies, bags of bubble gum, Spider-Man comic books for me, Strawberry Shortcake books for my sister. Dad would sometimes include a vintage baseball card — Hank Aaron, Willie Mays — after a trip to a baseball-card shop we'd discovered near our home in California. It would be an exaggeration to say Libby and I missed our parents during our summers at Gran's. Because Gran's house felt as much like home as our own did. But the care packages reminded us how much Mom and Dad loved us in a tangible, tightly packaged way. They made me miss them.

The first indication that this particular package was different was the fact that Libby's name wasn't on the brown paper Mom used to wrap it. Clearly big enough to hold a few surprises, the box was addressed to me. Just me.

I took the mail inside, scratched Bootsie on the back (anyone familiar walking through the door was a reunion to Bootsie), and went back to my room, a magazine and mysterious package in hand. The box was firm, and heavy enough to build suspense. I gently shook it but felt only slight movement from within. Time to end the drama.

Pulling back from a seam in Mom's wrapping, I saw a bright red box, with an all too familiar logo: Topps. Once the opening reached the other side of the package, the wrapper slid right off.

My gift was a full, factory-packed box of Topps baseball cards. The kind I'd normally see only at convenience stores (or baseball-card shops). Fold the lid back and within the box were 36 packs of baseball cards, each with 16 cards and a piece of the dry, flat, pink gum that had grown obligatory over the years. (If that gum left a mark on a prize baseball card, you might as well have rubbed the card in peanut butter.)

Dad had to be behind this. And it had to be a comforting gesture after Devon's death. 576 new baseball cards? Dad had long told me that buying more than four packs of baseball cards at a time was extravagant. (The first summer I collected, Granddaddy had taken me to the Hanky-Panky and cleared out the last 11 packs on the shelf. Drove my father nuts.) So here I have 36 packs in one fell swoop?

Mom and Dad were devastated by Devon's death. We'd talked about it over the phone, of course. Mom actually called three straight nights after first learning the news. She was as comforting as she could be from 2,000 miles away over a telephone line. And Dad tried to make me feel better, usually shifting the conversation to how the Cardinals were doing in the National League standings. Inevitably, the phone calls became long chats between Mom and Gran. How much centered around Devon . . . who knows?

This gift was Dad's way of helping me heal. A few days later during a visit with Auntie, she described the extravagant gift as a "heart-filler." ("Sometimes, Trey, our hearts grow a little empty," she said from her bed at Springview. "And those who love us are challenged with filling the emptiness. Those baseball cards are a heart-filler." She was right.) Counting the 3-D card of Ted Simmons Mrs. McGee gave me, my baseball card collection was growing by leaps and bounds since

Devon's death. He'd laugh at the irony of this.

In addition to filling my heart, that box of baseball cards became my first object lesson in self-discipline. Heeding my Dad's advice about the dangers of extravagance, I decided to open just four packs a day . . . for the next nine days. Few are the gifts we receive that last more than a week, but that box of 1982 Topps baseball cards sure did. Incidentally, I opened a pack with my favorite Cardinal — George Hendrick — on the seventh day. I planned on showing it to Arline so she'd remember how to pronounce his name.

18

"Uncle Herb's coming for supper!"

Libby's enthusiasm for guests knew no bounds. Her relationship with Herb Wilbury was primarily gathering quarters that Herb pretended he discovered in her ears. (He considered Libby too small to ride one of his horses, the protective instinct of a man with two daughters of his own.) But Herb made you smile. His visits for dinner at Gran's — always pork chops, fried okra, slaw, and corn bread — were highlights of our summer social calendar.

"Libby, would you please take the cole slaw out of the fridge? I've got four dishes there on the counter." Gran steadily monitored two skillets, one with sizzling, grease-popping pork chops; the other frying away her batter-slathered recipe for okra.

From the den, a Chattanooga news reporter updated viewers about the development of a new mall, mere prelude to Gran's daily weather update. ("Highs expected in the mid-nineties, humidity at 60 percent, with a chance of thundershowers in the afternoon." It was the same forecast, all summer. I never understood how the weatherman — Clark Randall — got paid. Easiest job on the planet.)

"I can smell it across town, Cooper!" Herb opened the front door like he lived here. "And I ain't sharin' those pork chops with anyone who calls himself a Cardinal fan!"

Gran smiled at Herb's entrance. There was nothing formal about greeting her country nephew. Even with all the volume he brought — maybe especially because of the volume — Herb belonged at Gran's. For visits.

"I saw the damnedest thing driving over here, Cooper." What followed was sure to be either a punch line or an observation of Herb's from atop a racist's tower of perception. "A colored woman pulled up next to me at the stoplight on a Harley! You ever seen such? Women ridin' motorbikes is foolish enough. But a colored girl?"

This was the dichotomy of Herb Wilbury. His alarm at seeing a woman on a motorcycle may have been rooted in concern for the well-being of a person riding a dangerous machine. (Not unlike his refusal to put my little sister atop a horse until she was bigger.) But then he shifts the tone of his concern toward the color of the rider's skin. Compassion wrapped in prejudice. Is that possible?

"I see all kinds of things downtown, Herb," said Gran, never taking her eyes from the stove top. "But I don't want these children riding motorcycles. No sir."

"Trey couldn't handle a Harley. Helmet would ruin that damn Cardinal cap!"

This was Herb's first dinner with us since Devon's death. The volume in Gran's kitchen felt good.

Herb had a curious habit at dinner time. One that all but ruined my appetite. One that had my sister's face contorting whenever Herb reached for his glass of milk.

Herb put cornbread in his milk.

Gran would cut him a square, just as she did for Libby and me, just as she did for herself. Brown on top, just this side of crispy. Yellow and soft beneath the crust . . . almost moist when she served the bread straight out of the oven.

But Herb would take his square, crumble it into pieces, and drop the pieces into his tall glass of milk. (Filled only halfway by Gran, who anticipated this bizarre cocktail as though her nephew were adding chocolate syrup in volume.) After every fourth or fifth bite of his pork chop, Herb would quaff this milk/bread mixture and — after swallowing — pause long enough to indicate how much he enjoyed his dinner beverage of choice. He smiled in answer to Libby's latest facial protest.

"Young lady, you look like you just stepped in a

169

terrier turd." This expression aggravated Gran, devoted to her Boston terriers.

"Language, Herb. Let the kids eat their supper."

"I'm really sorry about Devon, Trey. I know the two of you was close. He was a good boy, I could tell."

I wasn't used to a tone of compassion coming from Herb. The fact that it was spoken around bits of okra mashed between Herb's jaw and cheeks didn't reduce the comfort of the speaker's sentiment. "Devon knew how to behave. I don't like all kids, but I liked Devon McGee."

Herb meant most black kids, in his view, didn't know how to behave. And that he didn't like all black kids, but Devon was different. Still, this was powerful, coming from Herb, and at dinner time.

"He was indeed special," added Gran. "Last winter, I got sick. Could hardly get out of bed for a week with the crud." Like most Southerners, Gran called any illness that involved a runny nose or a cough "the crud."

"For some reason, my newspaper began showing up right outside the door, at the top of the steps." The paper was usually slung near the end of Gran's driveway, sometimes in the front yard, under her magnolia tree.

"Saved me having to walk clear to the street in

the cold to get my paper."

"Did the paper boy know you were sick?" Honest question from Libby.

"No, sugar. The paper carrier didn't even know if I was home or not." It wasn't a boy, and he drove a Chevy sedan. Slung the paper out the passenger-seat window. Gran felt closer to the city of Chattanooga than she did her carrier of the *News-Free Press*.

"But you know who did know I was sick?"

"Who?" Libby was now engrossed in the mystery.

"Devon McGee. On about the fourth or fifth day, I opened the door and saw Devon on that orange bike of his, leaving the driveway. With that newspaper at my feet. He had been biking over to move that paper a few feet closer to my door, helping my day start right. For the life of me, I don't know how or when he knew I was sick." Gran's eyes were getting damp as she tickled her okra with her fork. "He was indeed special."

* * *

Gran made coffee for Herb and poured a cup for herself. (Gran was a social coffee drinker. She preferred hot tea on her own.) She joined Libby in the living room to tackle the jigsaw puzzle Libby had poured out of a box a few days earlier. Libby called this endeavor "making picture pieces." Gran enjoyed

171

scenic puzzles: a winding country stream or maybe a bird's-eye view of a valley during fall, when the leaves make practically every piece of the puzzle a different color.

While the ladies were "making picture pieces," Herb and I sat down in the den for some TV time. It was Thursday night, which meant *Hart to Hart*. This was a detective show starring Robert Wagner and Stefanie Powers. Two actors older than my parents who somehow managed to retain their sex appeal. (Larry gawked at Powers' chest, of course. When I reminded him she's easily old enough to be his mom and, thus, could have breast-fed him, he actually recoiled. There weren't many layers to Larry.)

In this episode, the Harts — they were a detective team, but also a married couple — were investigating the disappearance of a jewelry-store owner's daughter. The owner — an elderly man — dismissed Mrs. Hart's role in the investigative partnership. A common theme on *Hart to Hart*. She would empower women — and attract a female viewing audience — but only after being slighted over the show's first half.

Herb sipped his coffee (loudly) and crossed his legs in the puffy, green, cloth-covered chair Granddaddy preferred. I sat where I always did, on the couch, across the room but with a direct view of

172

the TV. Bootsie hopped up next to me.

Looking at Herb, he reminded me of the black-and-white movies I'd catch Gran watching now and then. His face was taught, vertical lines descending from each side of his nose down to the base of his jaw. And the oil he put in his hair kept it slick and tight against his scalp, never a follicle out of place.

On these nights he'd visit for dinner, Herb Wilbury actually seemed to shine. And he seemed comfortable. I liked the volume of Herb at dinner time, and the quiet of our evenings together after dinner. Whether or not *Hart to Hart* was our entertainment of choice.

19

Chivalry is a process. An accidental process, and a slow one. The first time I bought something for a person of the opposite sex shouldn't stand out in my memory. That's not chivalrous, to remember the gift as a milestone.

But that's what it was, in fact. A milestone.

It had taken a couple of weeks, but Geraldine returned to the neighborhood, her chiming version of "When the Saints Go Marching In" growing gradually louder as she cruised the nearby streets. Libby had stopped her at the end of Gran's driveway a few days ago, and I followed my sister out, but just to see her. I know I'd stopped Geraldine for ice cream without Devon before, but it just felt different now. She stretched her cheeks to their limit with a smile and asked me where I'd been.

When I heard her this time, still a bit distant, I didn't wait for her to reach Gran's driveway. I grabbed a ten-dollar bill from my dresser drawer — the one with stacks of baseball cards still to be organized — and ran out the door to my bike. I needed a popsicle of some kind . . . and I needed a ride.

The sun blazing, it was the kind of afternoon that tested the freezing capacity of an ice-cream truck. At first faint, the jingle grew louder as I neared Terrace Lane. My pulse increased with proximity to this street, of course, and I turned left, pumping my pedals with some strain as I climbed toward the sound of Geraldine's truck.

And there it was, right where I feared . . . and right where I wanted that rolling freezer parked. Directly in front of Wendy's house. My skin already under a thin layer of sweat, I felt that brief-but-distinctive shot of adrenaline. Like the one I got every time I stepped into the on-deck circle of a Little League game. Was it excitement? Nerves? Dread? It was an emotional cocktail of some kind. And it had nothing to do with the selection of summer treats on the side of Geraldine's white truck.

And yep, there she was. After all, Geraldine only stops for customers. Wendy was gazing at those selections, a basketball under her left arm, as I pulled up on my bike.

"Hey, Trey." This was the first time I'd seen Wendy in the two weeks since Devon's funeral. The smile that accompanied her greeting was the first I'd seen from her in even longer.

"Hey, Wendy." She was sweating, too. Her hair was clinging to the sides of her head, tucked over her ears. Seeing her in a t-shirt (Braves again) and shorts made me feel foolish and somehow formal in my blue jeans. It was too hot for shorts, Gran told me every morning. They just made this encounter a touch more uncomfortable. But I was glad to be here.

Behind us, on the Nickersons' driveway, Jerry was taking jump shots with his own ball. (Having a father in the sporting-goods business meant an abundance of playing tools for Wendy and Jerry.) Shirtless, Jerry wore his maroon game shorts from Cleveland High.

I wondered if all varsity players get to keep their game shorts, or only the all-county sharpshooters. He had converse high tops, tied with maroon laces, giving Jerry the look of Muhammad Ali with his tasseled boxing boots. He wore a white head band to control his blonde hair, just long enough to be considered floppy. He was sweating more than Wendy or me, and it added to the picture of a budding athletic phenom. Even in August, I could picture Jerry bringing the Cleveland High gym to a roar with a last-second shot that hit nothing but twine.

"You playing hoops?" Small talk — even next to an ice cream truck — began with the obvious.

"Yeah. I'm kickin' his butt." Another smile. Tension eased further.

"What's it gonna be, kids? About time I see you out here, Trey. I know you've been missing your nutty buddies." Geraldine's smile felt as soothing as Wendy's. No mention of Devon from either of my friends and, honestly, I didn't want him brought up. Not now.

"I'll have a rocket pop, Geraldine." Wendy made the first call, and I had my breakthrough.

"Make it two." I spat the three words out before Geraldine could even turn from the window to get Wendy's selection. I'd seen Jack Tripper use this line in ordering drinks at the Regal Beagle in an episode of *Three's Company* just the day before. Earned him yet another date. Smooth.

"Well, awright then. Two rocket pops for the lady and gentleman." Did Geraldine wink at me?

Turning to Wendy, I caught her eyes, squinting in the sun. She was still smiling. Which strengthened my backbone the longer it lasted.

"Thanks, Trey. What's the occasion? I've got money, you know."

How do I answer? What *was* the occasion? The rare opportunity to do something nice for the girl who occupied my summer thoughts? A chance to spend some extra time with the girl who actually made me remember a funeral fondly? Or was it merely a 13-year-old inspired by a predictable

177

sitcom?

"Ahh, no occasion really. You can pick up the next round." That was my line: "the next round." Smooth.

"That's five dollars, Mr. California." Rocket pops were about the only item in Geraldine's truck that cost more than $1.50. Wendy had good taste in frozen treats. No cheap date here.

"Y'all be good now," said Geraldine. "Stay cool, but not too cool for more business tomorrow." She eased back onto Terrace Street, down the hill and a block closer to her next customer.

There's a reason rocket pops cost more than your average ice cream sandwich. They were essentially three layers of sweetened ice, red at the tip, white in the middle, blue at the bottom, near the stick. With vertical ridges, they actually looked like the kind of popsicle that could fly if launched properly. But they tasted too good for such a test.

"Jerry doesn't like ice cream?" He was dribbling feverishly, twenty feet from the basket. Looked more like a training session than a summer pick-up game with his kid sister.

"Football coach made the seniors swear off sweets. All summer." One more reason I'd reconsider a high school football career. "I like to eat popsicles in front of him."

I left my bike on the sidewalk and we walked along the driveway — around the basketball net — to Wendy's front porch. Sat down on the steps to make two rocket pops disappear.

"Where's Scary Larry?" I was eminently grateful, of course, that Larry Blackwell was *not* here. The entire scene would not have been possible, much less the one-on-one conversation time I was getting with Wendy. The fact that she coined him "Scary" made me feel even better. Wherever I might rank on the dial of Wendy Nickerson's romantic interests, it was ahead of "Scary Larry" Blackwell.

"Don't know." I wiped a drip of rocket pop — red? — from my chin. "Haven't seen him in a few days." Still no mention of Devon. Please, let's keep it this way.

"He's creepy sometimes, Trey. Jerry doesn't trust him. Says I need to stay wherever he isn't."

The fact that Jerry was protective of his sister inspired me. I'd like to think Libby cared about my view of things, and that, if warned, she'd stay away from the scary kids.

Watching Jerry drain one free throw after another — he was apparently in the cool-down mode of his session now — I felt like Wendy had the right eyes looking after her, even when mine were practically a continent away.

179

"Larry's harmless," I retorted. "A know-it-all who thinks he's in charge already, but harmless. Nothing to worry about."

"Does he ever talk about me?" Wendy now had a drip of rocket pop — white — on her chin. I desperately wanted to wipe it off, but she beat me to it.

"Sure, he talks about you." Larry talked about everybody, of course. Do I mention to Wendy that he typically starts with the subject of her chest? "Nothing really important; just talk." Did I just imply that Wendy isn't really important?

"That's really nice, you buying my rocket pop, Trey." She was watching her brother when she said this. Licking what remained of my noble purchase. "I guess this makes it a date."

I could feel the blood rush to my face. The sweltering heat had me somewhat flush, but Wendy Nickerson classifying the last ten minutes as a date had me in full blush. Felt like I was six years old and caught with a bag of cookies. Had to change the subject.

"You know, my basketball team went undefeated last season." Tafferty Junior High had gone 12-0 the winter before, easily winning our district championship. I'd made the team primarily because of my height — remember, I had all but reached my growth ceiling by my 13th birthday. I'd become a fairly dead-eye shooter by playing with my dad on our own driveway hoop, but my other skills — starting on the defensive end — kept me firmly planted to the bench for most of our unblemished season. My fellow bench-warmers had even come up with a nickname: The Pine Brothers. We had the best seats in the house, and the letters we were awarded at the end of the season were the same size and shape as those of the starters. We were hardly going to complain about playing time.

"I don't like basketball enough to play for a team," said Wendy. She loved soccer. And I knew she could throw a baseball better than Devon or Larry. "But it's fun to play with my brother. He says it develops his skills because he knows he can't be rough with me." Another note to myself: get Libby on the basketball court, or at least our driveway. Sibling bonds matter.

"Court's all yours." Jerry rolled the ball toward us and took off down the street. Had to wonder how long his training jogs were. The guy was good, and he was committed. And Wendy and I were now alone on her front steps.

"Let's play HORSE," she said. A pair of clean tongue-depressors were all that remained of our rocket pops. As Wendy picked up the basketball, I wiped my chin one more time.

Wendy's upper body bobbed when she dribbled, and she didn't take her eye off the ball. But she dribbled in command of the ball. Nothing timid. You can read a lot about a person's personality when you see them on a basketball court.

"Bank shot." She took her first shot from about five feet, a slight angle to the left of the rim. Indeed, it went in off the backboard, as called.

I took the ball, put one dribble between my legs, and kissed mine off the board and in.

"When do you have to go back home?" Wendy worded the question as though a return to my parents in California was an unwanted obligation. Standing in the midsummer heat with her — just the two of us in her driveway — the question was properly arranged.

"August 26th. It's a Saturday." I suppose the day of the week mattered.

"Cool . . . we've got lots of time." We.

She stepped up to the free-throw line her dad had painted, dribbled three times and shot. The ball collided with the heel of the rim and fell away. My shot.

Playing this very game with my dad in my own driveway back home, there was one shot I'd mastered. It's probably the shot that earned me my spot on that junior-high juggernaut at Tafferty.

There was a walkway that extended from our driveway to the front door of our house. If superimposed on a basketball court, the walkway would lead to the left corner, a spot on the floor for established shooters only.

From this angle, the backboard was no longer in play. A shot needed proper height and distance, measured precisely. If missed, the ball usually was an easy rebound for the opponent on the opposite side of the floor. But if made, it was the prettiest shot in the game. I became a deadeye standing in front of our doorway. That's what I was: a Doorway Deadeye.

As the Nickerson hoop was positioned (to the left side of the driveway), I had to stand on the sidewalk for this shot. As Wendy walked up to the basket, preparing to rebound, I took two dribbles, lifted the ball into shooting position just above my forehead, and released. Swish.

Wendy caught the ball before it hit the ground.

"Oooooh! Mr. California connects! On his way to the Lakers."

When Geraldine called me Mr. California, it sounded like derision. But I liked the tag as delivered by Wendy.

"That's my shot," I confirmed.

183

Wendy dribbled to the sidewalk — bobbing as her right hand controlled the ball — and turned for her attempt. "This is going in, Trey."

"Let's see it."

She used two hands when she shot. (Again, soccer was her game.) But she gave the ball arc, and managed some backspin (a shooter's touch). The ball hit the far side of the rim and fell toward the house. As I retrieved it, I wondered if the game was going in the direction I wanted.

"H," I announced. Unnecessarily.

"Give me the ball, Trey." She was standing in the same spot. Hands outstretched, awaiting the basketball. I tossed her a bounce pass.

"This is going in." She didn't dribble this time. Took the same two-handed shot, with a slight jump forward. The ball descended cleanly through the rim. This time, I caught it before it hit the pavement.

"It's my shot, too. Just needed one for practice."

She was competitive. And I loved this about Wendy. When she threw a baseball, she wanted it to pop into your glove harder than your throws hit hers. If riding a bike, she wanted to be at the front. A game of HORSE? She might concede the letter, but not the skill advantage. No way.

"Let's just shoot around," I said. I couldn't win in this dance. And I was smart enough to recognize it after one letter.

We played another 30 or 40 minutes. My jeans were clinging to my sweating legs. I wasn't brave enough to take my shirt off, especially after Jerry got back from his run, muscles gleaming that I wasn't convinced I had. He went inside for air-conditioned relief and a shower. As things seemed to be winding down, I asked Wendy a question I thought was harmless.

"What happened to your wrists?" There was slight bruising on both of Wendy's wrists, not as evident as they were at Devon's funeral, but still there.

She took a shot, rebounded the ball, and took another shot before replying.

"Nothing, really. I fell down. Tripped."

Too vague for the curiosity of a 13-year-old mind.

"Both wrists?"

"It's nothing, Trey. I fell down." When you hear your name included in an answer, it's code for "stop asking questions." I didn't know the code.

"Do they hurt?"

"Trey." My name again. "Does it look like they hurt? Would I be able to shoot baskets if my wrists hurt?"

My summer changed that day in Wendy's

driveway. The rocket pops and one-on-one basketball with Wendy was as perfect as a summer afternoon can be. It would be three weeks, though, before I knew why she was so sensitive about her wrist injuries. Wish I didn't know now what I didn't know then.

"I gotta go." If I had my way, I'd never leave. "Gran's probably wondering. Don't want to her to think I'm with Scary Larry."

The mention of her nemesis made Wendy smile. "Thanks again for the rocket pop, Trey. This was a good date."

As I picked up my bike, I wasn't blushing this time. It was a good date. With Wendy Nickerson.

20

Mom generally called on Thursdays. Looking back, I figure it must be because she and Dad took advantage of weekends for day trips. California is a day-tripper's fantasy.

When the phone rang on Thursday morning — midway through another *Three's Company* classic — I didn't even turn my head toward the phone. Jack was frantically preparing meals for two dates, one in his apartment, another upstairs in his neighbor's. At the same time. Classic.

Libby sprinted across the den and picked up the phone on the third ring.

"Hello, Johnson residence." My sister was precociously formal on the telephone. Surely impressed Mom.

"Yes. Here he is."

What the hell? I was distracted now. Libby wasn't talking with Mom. She had her right arm extended as far as the phone cord would reach in my direction. (Jack just dropped an entire bowl of pasta on his date upstairs. Classic stuff. Why does the phone ring when funny is happening?)

"It's Arline." Libby's face was expressionless, but she looked directly at me, awaiting a reaction. She enjoyed discomfort, whether it was Jack Tripper's or mine.

My heart climbed into my throat and seemed to throb there, making it ever so slightly harder to breathe. It was supposed to be Mom on the phone, asking about what books we were reading, or if we'd visited Auntie this week. Or what we ate for breakfast, for crying out loud. My heart didn't climb into my throat when Mom called.

"It's for you." As if Arline would call for Gran. As if Arline Varden — surely sitting in that trailer home, maybe on the couch where we watched the Braves-Phillies game — would call and ask for Libby Milligan. At that moment, though, I kind of wish she had. I could get back to Jack and his twin dates. Hmm. Twin dates.

I walked across the den and took the phone from Libby's hand. But I held the receiver at my side while Libby sprinted back to the couch to see how Jack survived his latest social stumble. Hmm. Social stumble.

I glanced into Gran's back yard, the sunshine begging me for another game of solo baseball. Then I sat down in Gran's swivel chair, next to the desk where the phone sat. What the hell? Mom always called on Thursdays.

"Hello."

"Hey. Whatcha doin'?" This wasn't going the direction I liked. Three words suggesting absolutely nothing, but not the direction I liked.

"Nothing. What's goin' on?" The question was asked not in the generalized, informal-greeting manner, but in a tone of literal curiosity. What's going on . . . this 12-year-old girl calling me in the middle of *Three's Company* when it should be my mom on the line? This girl who kissed me. This girl whose name, spoken by my sister, created an adrenaline surge like I was due up at the plate?

"The Twin Cinema is showing *Raiders of the Lost Ark* Saturday. You wanna go?"

Cleveland had two movie theaters, each with two screens. One of these was given the all-so-natural name, Twin Cinema. During the summer, the Twin would show classics on Saturday afternoons. And *Raiders of the Lost Ark* was already a classic. I'd seen it three times in that very theater the summer before when it was released. When Harrison Ford made me forget he'd ever played Han Solo. Best movie I'd ever seen. Or ever would see. Trouble is, I had told Arline it was the best movie I'd ever seen. Work yourself out of this one, Trey.

"Really? What time?" I knew the time. The

classic matinees were always at 2:00. The question bought my heart a few more resounding beats before I had to play this out.

"Two o'clock, I think. My mom will take us. Your grandma doesn't have to drive. Great movie. Isn't it cool they're showing it?"

Who is "they"? I wanted to know who was responsible for this set-up. Couldn't have been arranged by Arline alone. Not even with her mom's help. Hollywood was somehow behind this. I had no wiggle room.

"Yeah. Awesome." Did Arline think I meant her invitation was awesome?

"It's an awesome movie." Clarification.

"So is it a date?" I felt my cheeks flush. Phone on my right ear, heart uncomfortably rapid, the warm, fresh blood rushed to my cheeks and I blushed at Arline's eager inquiry. Two days after hearing Wendy use the word "date" with a smile, I had it thrown my way over telephone lines by another girl in my life. Twin dates.

There are times we pause for effect. In making an announcement that pleases us. ("I have chosen to attend college at . . .") Or announcing the winner of a game to the unaware. ("In the other semifinal . . .") Then there are times we pause simply because we're not sure we want to follow what next comes out of our mouth. I paused . . . *is it a date?*

"Sure. Sounds good. Indy's awesome." Hear that, young lady? Indiana Jones is awesome. He's the destination. He's the reason.

"Cool! We'll pick you up around 1:30. Don't bring Larry." Second girl this week to verbally reject Larry Blackwell. But in this case, it seemed like Arline was indeed ensuring this movie was . . . a date.

"Not enough blood for Larry," I said. Which was actually true.

"See you Saturday, Trey."

"Okay. Bye."

The end credits were rolling on *Three's Company*. Jack, Janet, and Terri walking through a zoo. A woman wrapped around each of Jack's arms. That was funny, right? One guy, two girls. Funny.

"Who was that, Trey?" Gran walked into the den. She'd been primping in her bedroom.

"It was Arline, Gran." Libby smiled as she told her, staring at me.

"Is everything okay? What did she want?" Gran turned from Libby to me.

"The Twin Cinema is showing *Raiders of the Lost Ark* on Saturday. She wants to go."

Gran stared at me. The silence lingered.

"With me. She wants to go with me."

More lingering silence. Gran turned to look at Libby, who was smiling to the point her eyes were squinting. As though she was suppressing a laugh.

Gran turned back to me. "Well . . . that sounds nice. Are you going?"

"I told her yes. That okay? We don't have plans, do we?"

"Why, no." Gran shook her head, pursed her lips, and looked at the floor. More silence. Lingering.

"Do we need to give her a ride, or are you meeting her at the theater?"

"She's picking me up. Well, her mom's driving. They're picking me up."

"Trey's going on a date." Libby nodded as she said this, looking at Gran for confirmation. Her smile was still there, but now under control.

"Well, hon, that's up to Trey, I suppose. Sounds to me like two friends going to see a good movie." Gran looked back at me, smiling herself now. And for the first time in my 13 years, I found myself wishing my grandmother would leave me alone.

Sure enough, she got up and headed for the kitchen. "Saturday afternoon, right?"

"Yep."

Libby got up, too. She was too smart to stay in the den, alone with me, after adding her commentary to the breaking news.

"It's not a date," I said, just loudly enough for Libby to hear as she left the room.

21

Summer days offer the illusion that they'll never end. This goes for the season itself — three months free of alarm clocks, assignments, or deadlines — and for the individual days, as units of boundless time. It's a time when looking forward to something specific — an event, a trip, *a date* — is silly, as every summer moment becomes its own reward. There's nothing to overcome, or get by, during summer. Nothing to endure.

Likewise, it's hard to dread anything specific — an event, a trip, *a date* — during the summer. Because time seems slower, so many blanks to fill as one day blends into another. Next Tuesday may get here . . . it may not. Three weeks from now? Beyond the reach of a boy's mind. A date — with a girl — tomorrow, Saturday? This being Friday, there's nothing to worry about.

Gran dropped me off at Springview to have lunch with Auntie while she and Libby did some clothes shopping. Gran would buy new clothes for me and have me try them on at the house, knowing I was easy to please. She merely needed to get the size right as my arms and legs stretched new limits. But with Libby, she needed to raise a smart shopper. Having me impatiently monitor such an outing was counterproductive on a few levels. A few hours with Auntie were a welcome alternative.

I took a box of baseball cards with me for these visits. Auntie liked to watch CNN — she kept her TV on the relatively new 24-hour information network every waking hour, hitting the mute button when visitors stopped by. I liked to sort my cards on the small coffee table next to her bed.

One of the things I loved most about Auntie was the way she relished the companionship of family, but didn't feel compelled to fill every minute with conversation. "Silence can be a virtue," she often reminded me. Especially when Libby got a bit chat-happy.

We'd finished lunch — sliced turkey, corn, green beans, and a brownie — and were settling back into virtuous silence when a segment came on the air about trouble in the House of Windsor. Something about Charles, the Prince of Wales, squabbling with Diana, his wife only since the previous summer. I hadn't learned a thing about tabloid journalism to this point in my life, which means my clarity of thought was probably at its peak. Auntie seemed surprised that such a story would make the desk of a CNN talking head.

"I wish they'd leave those two alone," she said. She shook her head; looked more concerned than I would have expected. Auntie had a healthy perspective on life's blessings. She had methods for avoiding frustration, anger, and worry. "Life's too short." Another of her mantras.

"Didn't they just get married last year?"

I had actually risen in the middle of the night with Gran to watch some of Charles and Di's wedding ceremony. Disney come to life, Gran had said. We shouldn't miss it.

"Just last year, that's right. A good marriage takes time, Trey. Doesn't help if your kitchen quarrels get broadcast all over the world."

The report alluded to the couple not having been seen in public for more than six weeks. I wondered if there was a minimum duration for public appearances by a royal couple. Or the absence of public appearances.

"What are they quarreling about?"

"That's just it, Trey. We don't know. Those reporters don't know. Jim Riggins certainly doesn't know." Jim Riggins was the CNN talking head sharing this news.

"It's speculation and rumor, Trey. Innuendo. Know what that means?"

I nodded my head. But I hadn't the foggiest idea

what innuendo meant.

"Matters of the heart are not news. At least, they shouldn't be news, Trey. A love letter is between two people, and two people only. And a quarrel between a married couple is a quarrel between two people. Only."

"How did you know Uncle was the right one, Auntie?" I'd never met the man my mom called "Uncle." He had died a few years before I was born.

Auntie smiled, only slightly. That smile of recognition. I'd tossed her an easy question.

"I'll tell you how you know you have the right partner, Trey. Are you paying attention?"

I nodded.

"I knew Uncle was the right one when he was the man I wanted to be with when I was feeling the worst. A sad afternoon. A frustrating week. A lonely weekend. When I was at my lowest, Uncle was the one person who could pick me up. Without fail. That's how I knew he was 'the one,' as you say."

I nodded. "You must have wanted to be with him when you're happy, too."

"Oh, of course. Of course, Trey. My happiest moments were with Ed Caldwell. To this day, those moments are countless, and they bring a smile to my face. But hear me on this: it's easy to fall in love when you're happy. Enjoying a person's company when the birds are singing, the check's in the mail, and your ball team is winning . . . that's easy. But who will you call on when times are rough? When sorrow hits? That's the person you should marry.

"I sometimes wonder if Charles and Diana gave themselves time to experience sorrow together. Before getting married, I mean. Seems they may have found their way to it."

Auntie was a wise woman. I liked my time with her. The rest of our visit was rather silent. Couldn't bring myself to mention my "date" with Arline. Or Wendy Nickerson. But I was thinking about the girls in my life under an entirely new light. Auntie was better than CNN.

* * *

The nerves hit at breakfast Saturday. Gran cooked link sausages and scrambled eggs. Libby opened a new box of Apple Jacks. And I pondered the coming event as though it were an oral report in front of Mr. Butler's science class back home. So much for the boundless time of summer.

"Can I go to the movie, Gran? I like Indiana Jones." Libby had good taste in archaeologists, but no sense of what "third wheel" meant.

Gran kept her eyes on the sausage as grease spat above the pan, the smell — and some smoke — filling the kitchen even as the air conditioner strained to keep things cool and comfortable.

"I need you to be my shopping partner, Sugar." She said *shuggah*, as every grandmother in the American South did.

"But why doesn't Trey have to be a shopping partner?"

I glared at Libby, despite the thought that I'd actually be more comfortable at the grocery alongside my grandmother than I'd be in a dark theater with Arline Varden. Maybe I could trade places with my sister. Arline's mom pulls up, and I shove Libby out the front door. That would put a twist on things.

"Well. Trey's got a . . . ." Gran was still facing the stove top. This was my first experience with what I learned to call a *pregnant pause*. The word that forced Gran to tap her verbal brakes was, of course, "date."

"Trey's been invited to the movie, Lib. It wouldn't be right for you to invite yourself along."

"Is Arline's mom taking you?"

Libby had her claws around my discomfort. It may have been involuntary, a young sibling of the opposite sex feeling her way through a rite of passage she'd have to hurdle herself someday. But she wouldn't hurdle it as blindly as her big brother.

"Libby, mind your own business, okay? You've seen the movie. It's no big deal."

"Then why do you want to see it again?"

Gran turned at this inquiry, lifting the pan away from the heated coil. The sound of grease spitting began to soften. Which made this conversation seem that much more dramatic.

"I want to see it because it's a classic." Gran placed a plate in front of me, eggs and three glistening sausage links.

"And because Arline asked you, right?" I could actually see my 8-year-old sister suppressing a grin. There was nothing involuntary about this interrogation. Libby was loving it.

"Who wants some orange juice?" Gran was pouring as she asked, which means the question was a red light between two conversational cars on track for a head-on collision.

"I don't want to talk about this any more," I said, stuffing half a link into my mouth and reaching for my glass of O.J.

Truth is, I didn't know if Arline's mom would be going to the movie with us or merely acting as chauffeur. Libby's question only complicated my discomfort. And four hours remained till my first date was to commence.

I played baseball, as I did every day. But my mind wasn't on a batting order, or the score. The rhythmic throw-bounce-catch helped distract my body, but my mind was wandering with worry. A few years later, such a practice would be described by my coach as "going through the motions." Body doing one thing, mind elsewhere. Going through the motions indeed.

The only time a child watches a clock is near the end of a school day. You've seen *Risky Business*, when an impatient, frustrated young pimp played by Tom Cruise watches as the minute hand on a clock actually moves backward as it nears bell time. As my date with Arline approached, I watched Gran's clocks.

Sorting baseball cards in my room, it was the digital clock next to my bed. Watching TV, it was the clock above Gran's desk . . . Roman numerals, the minute hand advancing in the proper direction, and all too quickly. Clockwise, and quickly.

Gran gave me a twenty-dollar bill, folded cleanly right between Andrew Jackson's eyes. "Have fun, Sugar." *Shuggah*.

"Treat Arline to a drink, you hear?"

My pulse quickened that much more. A new expectation for this event, this palm-sweating interruption to my summer escape, a thousand miles from all the things that should make me nervous. Two hours in the dark with this girl . . . and the drinks on me?

Beep-beep! Two quick notes from the driveway. (It was only 1:28!) I grabbed my Cardinal hat from the arm of the couch where Bootsie was napping. (Dogs never worry about dates. I actually pondered this as I put my hat on.) Gran beat me to the door, but only peeked through the glass. Idling at the end of the driveway was Theresa Varden's olive-green two-door Pontiac. Inside — barely visible from Gran's front door — the first and most significant social challenge of my 13-year-old life. I could tell Arline had her hair in a pony tail. And she was sitting in the back seat. Yep . . . this was a date. As I felt Gran pat the top of my head and I stepped toward that Pontiac, I wondered what Wendy would think of the scene. The thought didn't help my nerves.

22

"Hey there, Trey!!" Arline's mom shouted at me as she leaned across the front seat to shove the massive passenger door open. Once open, I recognized the first awkward moment of the afternoon. With Arline in the back seat — she slid across the seat so that she was directly behind her mom — I had to move the front seat forward (there was a lever on the side) so that I could slide into the rear chamber with my love interest. That is, squeeze into the back seat with the first girl who ever kissed me. That is, get in the stinkin' car!

"Hey. Thanks for picking me up, Ms. Varden."

Once in the back seat, I couldn't reach the passenger door handle. Arline's mom got out of the car, walked around the front — waving at Gran, still standing in the doorway — and shut the door with a slam that rocked me another inch closer to my date. To Arline.

"How's it goin'?" She was wearing a black, sleeveless top, with a single yellow flower in the center. And blue jeans. The flower seemed small, more an accessory to her shirt than a decoration. Arline looked nice.

"Good. I'm good. How are you?" Adjusted my cap. Pulled it a little lower. I should have worn sunglasses. To a movie. Yeah, sunglasses would have helped.

As we backed out of Gran's driveway, I noticed Arline's mom had a cigarette clamped just inside the left side of her mouth. She squinted, like smokers do, as she steered the car onto the street. "Indiana Jones, you best get ready!" Ms. Varden made up for my nervousness with enthusiasm. She was a loud, vibrant, smoking ice-breaker.

"I love this movie," said Arline. "Wish they'd make another one." Word was a sequel would hit screens next summer.

"I'm sure they will. I guess Harrison Ford has to take turns between *Star Wars* and Indy. Wouldn't want Han Solo showing up on an archaeological dig." Humor from the anxious Cardinal fan.

"That would be hilarious. What if Chewbacca came out of nowhere to rescue Indy. Or C3-PO started lecturing Nazis!" Humor from my date. I smiled. They were funny images, to be sure.

"What's Larry up to?" asked Arline.

"I haven't seen him in a while." I really hadn't. Probably a week since we'd even talked on the phone.

"You and Larry hang out a lot?" Ms. Varden

looked up into the rearview mirror, right at me.

"Yeah, I guess so." The truth.

"What does that boy like to do?" A more challenging question than I would have thought.

"You know, the usual stuff," I said.

"Does he play any sports?"

"Not really." Devon and I would shoot hoops with Larry and he wouldn't so much as touch the ball. And he didn't like bikes.

"Is he in Boy Scouts?" Where did that come from? I wasn't in Boy Scouts.

"No, I don't think so."

"I never see him at the pool." Cleveland had a municipal swimming pool. I hardly ever went; only when distant cousins came to visit Gran. And judging by Larry's tan (what's the opposite of tan?), he never went to a pool.

"Mom, it's up ahead." Arline pointed to the marquee, just beyond a big Arby's sign. In black, block letters, there were but two words: "Tootsie" and "Raiders." I loved the fact only one word was needed to tell Cleveland about this blockbuster encore. And I chuckled at the lunacy of anyone considering a film called *Tootsie* when Indiana Jones was saving the world next door.

Ms. Varden drove the car right up to the sidewalk in front of the theater. She reached over and

205

shoved the passenger door open, so her daughter and I could get out safely away from parking-lot traffic.

"You kids have a blast! I'll be back in two hours. You got a dime, Arline?" In case of an emergency call, kids carried dimes.

"I've got a dime." Arline slid over and out of the car, as I held the folded passenger seat down.

"Thanks for the ride, Ms. Varden." I slammed the door shut. The car rocked gently. It was a massive door.

"Hey, one more thing," said Ms. Varden. "No holding hands!!" She laughed a smoker's laugh (grinding gravel inside her throat), and slowly pulled away. I know I was blushing, but the Cardinal cap helped. It was even more red.

The air conditioning of the cinema hit us almost as powerfully as the smell of popcorn. This sensory cocktail was among my favorites, and as distinct to my summers in Cleveland as the sound of my rubber baseball slamming against Gran's patio wall. Arline was smart to wear blue jeans. The shorts I had on would have my knees freezing before Indy escaped that giant boulder. Oh well. I'd come to my share of movies at the Twin Cinema. But not many matinees, during the day when I was outside. In shorts. My bare legs. Arline's bare arms. Quite a tandem.

The lobby was crowded. Mostly kids. A few parents with an excuse to see a movie they loved but weren't comfortable admitting they loved. There was comfort in the number of people, until I realized I had to keep track of where Arline was. And make sure I was next to her. Like a couple on a date.

"Want popcorn?" She was looking back at me as she started toward the back of one of the concession lines.

"Yeah, I guess so." No way was I watching Indiana Jones without popcorn.

Standing in line, staring up at the prices for junk food and soda, I found myself wishing Devon were here. But if he were, he'd be suppressing laughter the entire time. He'd have had me blushing far more than this date of mine. Still, I found myself wishing he were here.

"I'll get the drinks." Gran had given me that extra five dollars. I owed Arline a soda.

"Okay. Thanks. That's cool, Trey." Arline's mom made the best milk shakes in Tennessee. The least I could do is buy Arline a soda.

"One medium popcorn." That's a lot of corn for one girl, I thought.

"Butter?" Why is butter a question for movie popcorn? Isn't butter what makes movie popcorn . . . *movie popcorn?*

207

"Yes, please."

Arline stepped aside, cradling her tub of popcorn. "I like Sprite."

"Two small Sprites and a small popcorn." I liked Sprite, too.

"*Trey!*" What did I do?

"What?"

"I got this for *both* of us!" No way was I watching Indiana Jones without my own popcorn. And, while I'd buy Arline a drink with Gran's money, I wasn't going to share a tub of popcorn with her. Nope. That was intimate.

I stared at Arline, my mouth slightly open, as though I was stumbling with my response to her popcorn clarification. In fact, I was stalling long enough for the popcorn guy to get back with my bag full. Too late to correct the error.

"Butter?"

"Yes, please."

* * *

Looking back, the image is funny. Arline and I, walking toward the theater entrance in tandem, my date — a year younger, and six inches shorter — carrying a popcorn container twice the size of the one in my left hand. She actually had to hug the tub of corn while holding her Sprite. Devon would have loved this. But it was actually me suppressing a smile.

Through the dim lighting of the theater, we were able to scan the rows for a pair of vacant seats. And there weren't many left. Arline took the lead and, turning sideways, shuffled down a row about five from the back of the theater. Though slightly to the right of center, they were great seats. As packed as this place was, we couldn't have done better.

The chick with the massive popcorn tub earned a stripe. I sat down to Arline's left, immediately to the right of an overworked mother. (The woman appeared to have at least four kids with her. I wondered how much of the movie she'd actually see.)

Let's face it: a movie theater is a terrible place to get to know someone. You can't talk to each other. You're expected to stare straight ahead — at the screen — so you can't look at each other. And if you did look at each other, it's too dark to really see your date's eyes.

A movie theater silences you, blinds you, and immobilizes you. Somehow, it's the venue for more first dates than anywhere else. Munching on still-warm popcorn, awaiting Indy's next big escape, the venue was perfect for this first date. I was with Arline Varden . . . but I wasn't.

Midway through the film, it happened. More subtle than that kiss of several weeks ago, but every bit as startling.

There's a scene where Belloq — Indy's rival and a Nazi sympathizer — allows a kidnapped Marion to share a drink with him. In his tent where Belloq's men are digging in search of the Ark. Marion turns the table on Belloq by luring him into a drinking contest.

Just as Marion downed a shot of some liquid fire, Arline turned the table on me by grabbing my right hand as it dangled off the end of our shared armrest. My popcorn long gone, my Sprite on the floor next to my left foot, I had sat idle for several minutes. Long enough for Arline to slide her left hand inside my right.

I stared at the screen. Belloq was laughing, drunk enough to be silly. No way would I turn and look at Arline now. But I held her hand. Not tightly. But I held it. Felt my heart pound more deeply. And I blushed. Bless the darkness of a movie theater. I blushed, blood filling my cheeks and ears, a sense of perspiration on my brow. But she'd never know. Arline had my hand, I had hers, and we both still had Indiana Jones.

Chase scenes aren't for hand-holding, though. Whether it was five minutes later or twenty, who cares? By the time Indy was hopping between (and under) Jeeps in pursuit of his treasure, Arline and I had disengaged. The separation was mutual, and happened naturally. Chase scenes aren't for hand-holding. Arline knew this.

Our attention — all of it — was back to the screen, right up to that final scene in the warehouse, the Ark of the Covenant tucked neatly amid the countless other discarded tokens of human achievement.

Roll the credits.

Back in the lobby, Arline and I walked to the front, the glass wall keeping the cool air in and allowing us a view to the parking lot as we scanned for Ms. Varden.

"I need to go to the bathroom," said Arline.

I nodded. Still hadn't spoken since we returned to the well-lit world.

"Hey, Trey."

For at least the third time in the last two hours, my heart jumped in my chest. Pounding rhythmically inside my ribcage, wanting to burst free.

"Are you here with Arline?"

Wendy.

"Hey . . . Wendy." Fighting a blush. That sweat on my brow. Again.

"What a great movie. I didn't know you were coming."

Jerry — Wendy's brother, his shirt on today — was a few feet behind her, talking with a feather-haired brunette. I didn't know guys like Jerry even went to matinees, much less with dates.

"I came with Jerry and Julie." The alliterative bond between Wendy's brother and his girlfriend seemed as natural as bread and butter.

"Cool. Yeah . . . it's a great movie. Probably my favorite."

"You came with Arline?"

"Uhhh . . . yeah. I needed a ride." Here came the lies.

"Who else came?"

"Actually, it's just Arline and me. Her mom drove us." Like Gran didn't have a driver's license.

"Just you and Arline. That's, like, a date." Wendy smiled at this. Big. Beautiful smile.

"It's not a date." Full blush now. But it felt okay. Wendy had poked my ribs, as it were. Blushing was safe.

"Did you ask her?"

"She called. She asked me. I needed a ride." That lie. Again.

"That's nice."

"Hey, Wendy." Arline was back. Now she was

smiling. Big.

"Hey, Arline. Nice of you to give Trey a ride."

Arline looked at me. And kind of tilted her head. I've seen that look too many times, from too many girls and women since that afternoon. Translation: "What nonsense are you uttering now?"

"I'll see you around." Wendy half-raised her right hand. Not quite a goodbye wave, but not exactly a one-arm dismissal. I'm not sure what kind of gesture it was. But I didn't like it.

"There's my mom," said Arline, pointing toward the curb in front of the theater. My eyes stayed on Wendy, walking off into the crowded lot next to her brother and his date.

24

Summer rain storms — at least those in the American South — are like unruly relatives. Rarely seen, and when seen, often brief. But always loud. And always disruptive.

Rainy days at Gran's meant game after game of Crazy Eights. The only item Gran kept on her kitchen table that wasn't directly related to serving (or eating) food was a deck of cards. Gran and I gravitated to that table on rainy days, when I couldn't play my brand of baseball in the backyard. While Libby occupied herself with dressing and undressing her dolls, Gran and I played Crazy Eights. And we talked.

Gran liked Crazy Eights because it was a game more about random luck than clever strategy, experience, or guile. The idea wasn't to beat me, but to spend time with her grandson. (And granddaughter. Libby joined us sometimes and could match suits and numbers as well as Gran or me.) She won plenty of games. I won plenty of games. However steady the rain, however window-rattling the thunder, the stormy days at Gran's house became some of my favorites.

"Who are the Cardinals playing tonight?" Gran asked the question with a cigarette clamped inside the left corner of her mouth. I've seen gangsters (in movies) less adept at talking while smoking than my grandmother.

"The Reds, in Cincinnati." I stared at my hand while Gran placed four consecutive cards. When she finally had to draw, she tapped her cigarette in the clear glass ashtray she kept in the kitchen. An ashtray bigger than my cereal bowl.

"The Reds. That's Pete Rose and Tommy Bench, right?" Gran knew her Atlanta Braves. But details among other National League clubs escaped her.

"No. Rose is with the Phillies now." And had been for three years. "And it's Johnny Bench. He's still their catcher. Always will be." (Bench retired after the 1983 season.)

"Johnny Bench. That's right."

If cigarettes were Gran's vice, mine was grape Nehi. Best soda pop on the planet, and made better by the ribbed bottles in which they were delivered. There was one place in Cleveland that served grape Nehi: the Texaco station (two blocks from the Hanky-Panky) where Gran filled her Buick's tank. You could only buy one at a time, for 35 cents, from the ancient vending machine inside the station's front door. A lock-and-release system that made you feel like you'd either remove the bottle from the machine — neck first — or lose your hand trying. Gran would let me buy four at a time when she got a fill-up. I came to see a quarter and a dime as a magical marriage.

When playing Crazy Eights, grape Nehi was my elixir. Made me love Gran that much more, however smoky her kitchen became.

"Well, Trey, how was your afternoon with Arline?"

Rain. Thunder. A question from my grandmother about a girl. I took a gulp from my Nehi. And I stared at my hand. No match.

"It was fine." Still staring at my hand. Still no match.

"I know you enjoyed the picture." Gran was of that generation that still called movies "pictures."

"Did you treat Arline to her drink?"

"Yeah. I did."

"I know she appreciated your generosity. You're a young gentleman, Trey." Gran puffed on her cigarette, exhaled the smoke, and smiled at me.

I drew a card.

"Tell me about Arline; she's so friendly. But what kinds of things does she enjoy? Isn't she a baseball fan?"

"She likes the Braves." I felt the beginning stages of a blush, a flashback to the kiss. Wondered if every

216

time I said the word "Braves" I'd have this reaction. Didn't know the word *Pavlovian* yet.

"Nothing wrong with being a Braves fan." Gran winked at me and took another drag on her cigarette. Bob Horner and Dale Murphy were her favorites. I knew that.

"She thought the Cardinals' rightfielder is George Hendrix."

"And what's wrong with that?"

"Gran . . . his name is George *Hendrick*. He leads the team in home runs. He deserves to have his name pronounced right."

Gran chuckled, and put the cigarette down in her giant ash tray. Not quite ready to be extinguished.

"I'm glad you take your Cardinals so seriously, Trey. There's no sense in following a team if you're not going to pay attention to the details. And do so with passion. You're right: a name should be pronounced correctly, especially if the player is special. Like George . . . Hendrick."

Gran had discarded four cards, and was down to three. In discarding three of my own, I still had six in hand.

"If you think about it, Trey, cheering your favorite baseball team is not all that different from taking care of a girlfriend. Details matter. A lot."

"She's not my girlfriend, Gran. Not even close."

"I'm not saying Arline is your girlfriend, sugar. Not at all. But if you're going to have dates with a girl now and then — and Trey, you are going to have dates — a few tips from your old grandmother might come in handy. Before I met your granddaddy, I went on some good dates . . . and some bad ones. I'd rather you be remembered years from now as a good date. By Arline and any other lucky young lady you might court."

Court. Gran made it sound like I was below a balcony, Arline calling my name into the moonlight. The conversation wasn't going to end quickly enough. So I shifted gears to my advantage. At least to what I thought was my advantage.

"How do I recognize a good date, Gran? Let's say I do all the right things, pay attention to all the right details. How will I know if the girl is a good date?"

Now Gran did snuff out her cigarette. Without taking a last puff. She was considering this question seriously.

"Well now. That's a deep question, young man." Gran usually called me "young man" when I was being admonished. In this case, she seemed to be establishing a new tone. I *thought* the shift was to my advantage.

218

"Girls can be complicated dates, Trey. What they enjoy — and what they don't like — is not always easy to recognize . . . and never on a first date. A girl will smile and go along with almost any suggestion a gentleman makes on that first date. A polite girl will. But a boy won't know if it's genuine or not until he asks for that second date."

"Why won't she just tell him if she likes an idea or not?" We began referring to "she" and "him" as though they were characters in a story. Which I suppose they were.

"It's a first date, Trey. It's not so much about having fun — doing what one likes — as it is about learning what someone else likes. A smart girl does more studying on a first date than she does anywhere outside a classroom."

Had Arline been studying me at that movie? No chance.

"What about asking someone to a first date?" My heart rate elevated a bit here, as I had someone in mind. Someone who made my heart rate elevate.

"I don't know if I can help you much there, sugar. I never asked a boy on a date, believe it or not. When I was young, that was not something a girl did. Not a polite girl. She waited for the boy to ask her. And let me tell you, I was so pleased when your grandfather asked me on our first date. It was just for

219

lunch, a diner near the warehouse where he worked. I was his lunch break that day." Gran smiled and looked down at the last two cards in her hand. I didn't know what to say; just that I missed Granddaddy, too.

Gran looked up, directly into my eyes.

"There are two types of girls, Trey. Your mother would insist I'm being too narrow in saying this. But it's something I believe."

I discarded one card, but was stuck with five.

"There are girls who are eager. Eager to learn, eager to please, eager to explore. They are curious about you, Trey. And they want to find their way into your world. These girls can be intimidating, even when they're younger than you."

Arline.

"And there are girls who are mysterious, Trey. They're harder to know, harder to get close to. They'll force you to explore, Trey. They'll make you curious. Younger, older, it doesn't matter. Those you find gorgeous — beyond nice hair and a pretty smile — will fit this type, Trey. They'll be mysterious."

Wendy.

Gran placed an eight of clubs on the discard pile. Her hand was empty.

25

I'm not into foreshadowing. I've come to see things related only as much as a person allows them to be related. If you wear a certain t-shirt and your team wins . . . great. Nice to associate that shirt with a happy moment. But did the shirt on your body help your team to victory? Nah.

So the fact that Gran and I played Crazy Eights on August 7th had nothing to do with August 8, 1982, being the scariest brush with fate of my life (before or since). I haven't been fond of the number eight since that day. And I never played Crazy Eights with Gran again.

Sundays were for backyard baseball. This one was sweltering before the sun even climbed above the tree line behind Gran's house. With no *Three's Company* — once a week, nearly every channel was devoted to local and not-so-local preachers — Libby and I were outside as soon as we finished our Rice Krispies. I was striking out L.A. Dodgers. Libby was making herself a distraction.

"When are you gonna bat?"

I hurled another pitch at the patio wall as Libby stood atop the four-foot platform, leaning over the rail like a heckling fan. Fielded the rebound cleanly and threw it back at the wall — my first baseman, Keith Hernandez — for the first out of the second inning.

"When are you gonna bat?"

A purely nonsensical question from my 8-year-old sister. Until I considered the game of baseball as she (and every other 8-year-old in America) understood it.

"How am I gonna bat, Libby? Who's gonna pitch?"

"I will."

I took the signal from my catcher (Darrell Porter), wound up and delivered. *Thwap*. Fielded the rebound to my backhand, planted my right foot, and threw another seed to Hernandez. Out two.

"You can't pitch, Libby. And we don't have a bat."

"But you keep score, don't you?"

I missed *Three's Company*.

"Yes, I keep score."

"Well then, how do you score points?"

"Runs, Libby. You score runs in baseball. There are no points."

"How do you score runs?"

I ignored the impulse to throw my rubber baseball directly at Libby's nose, wound up, and hurled another fastball at the patio wall. The rebound skipped along the still-damp grass . . . and bounced off the heel of my glove. Error, Milligan. Dodger safe at first base.

"Just don't worry about it, Libby." My fallback conversation-ender when it came to my sister. *Just don't worry about it, Libby.*

This is when my day changed for the worse. Much worse.

Gran slid open the glass door and leaned out.

"Larry's on the phone, Trey."

Only Larry Blackwell would make a phone call before noon on Sunday. This was the kind of "little thing" that bothered Gran so much about him. But instead of ignoring the phone, or slamming it down after educating Larry, Gran called me in to see what could possibly be so urgent on everyone else's Day of Rest. Gran even got angry gracefully.

"Hello?"

"Hey Trey. Let's catch some crawdaddies."

The worst day of my first 14 years (hell, the worst day of all my years) began innocently enough. Larry and I had gone on crawdad hunts — in the stream we called Crawdad Creek — a dozen times since we'd met two summers ago. So his invitation was no more significant than a request to play catch in Gran's backyard (as if Larry would even consider such). The invitation was much *less* significant than Arline's. Catching crawdads didn't make me blush.

"Yeah, alright," I told Larry. "I'll be there in a minute." I hung up the phone and looked into the kitchen, where Gran was looking back at me, over the stove. She knew Larry, of course. And she knew this was Sunday morning. The two didn't mix well.

"What's young Mr. Blackwell up to this morning?" She asked this as she grabbed a coffee mug from the dishwasher, rubbing the already dry vessel with a nearby rag.

"He wants to catch some crawdads. Okay if I go?"

I hadn't seen Larry since July had turned to August. Gran may have been holding out for September.

"Awfully early for a Sunday, Trey." I looked at the clock, which said 11:41. Anything before noon on Sunday was awfully early to Gran.

"Should I wait a while?" Nineteen minutes would do it.

Gran put the coffee mug in its proper cabinet and reached into the dishwasher for another. Without looking up, she said, "Go ahead. You two have fun. Stay out of trouble."

Stay out of trouble.

* * *

I secured my already-damp-from-sweat Cardinal cap, put a wrist band on my left arm — this was somehow cool when riding a bike — and pedaled down Gran's driveway toward calamity. The day was humid and getting more so. It was hot and getting hotter. The elements seemed to be conspiring with my pal, Larry. But neither he nor I knew it yet.

A coating of sweat covered me when I pulled into Larry's driveway. Climbing the hill to Larry's house — the hill that Cleveland's well-to-do called home — was a workout I welcomed. One Larry wouldn't — probably couldn't — tackle with me. His house's proximity to Gran's — and the homes' relative elevation — reflected our relationship in more ways than one. For Larry, a lazy convenience. For me, a steep hill climb.

"I got the jars." Larry leaped off his front porch, hurdling three steps to the front walkway. He did so with a one-gallon pickle jar under each arm. Calamity was in the air; we just didn't know it.

Despite the heat, Larry was wearing blue jeans and a black t-shirt with the band Journey's logo silk-screened on the front. Something his mom had gotten him at a concert not that long ago. I don't think Larry was aware how uncool Journey was to most guys our age. If hard rock described my

225

preferences, Journey was the prototype for soft rock. Larry didn't care.

"How ya been, man?" Larry handed me one of the jars, I propped my bike next to his garage, and we walked down the Blackwell driveway toward the dead end of innocence.

I never learned if Crawdad Creek was the official name of the meandering stream that served as our version of Huck Finn's Mighty Mississippi. (I do know Huck was in a lot better hands with Jim than I was with Larry Blackwell.)

The creek — no more than five feet wide or two feet deep at flood stage — served essentially as a moat below the wooded hill that separated Larry's neighborhood from that of the smaller, two-bedroom homes on Cleveland's outskirts. Higher ground meant higher property values. That's what Larry claimed at least. A mantra he'd obviously heard his father repeat at the dinner table. As though the rabble of Cleveland could storm the gates at the next tax increase. Higher ground. And Crawdad Creek.

The particular spot we liked was actually through a clearing in the woods. As long as we'd hunted crawdads, this clearing had been our grounds. We had to descend a steep, wooded hill just across the street from Larry's house. On the other side of the creek was a clearing about the size of a

226

Little League infield. Why the trees had been removed in this spot . . . who knows. A rim of pine trees enclosed us and provided just enough cover from a recently developed neighborhood of small homes. Through those pine trees, you could glimpse the bright yellow of a backyard swing set. Maybe the sun's reflection off the chrome of another Buick's bumper. But the homes were a football field away.

These were our grounds.

"Damn! Look, Trey. There's an army in here!!"

Larry had the lid of his jar off, the vessel half-filled with water that can best be described as the color of drainage from a can of blackeye peas. He plunged his hand into the slow current and came up with the first catch of the day.

"Beauty!"

A crawdad is a redneck's lobster. Properly called crayfish, they have pincers, like a lobster. Tentacles, like a lobster. A body divided into two sections, like a lobster. And if you're just redneck enough, you can eat the tail. Like a lobster. Butter optional. I've yet to taste my first crawdaddy, but I've caught hundreds of them.

"Sumbitch!" One of the things Larry loved most about Crawdad Creek was the lifting of any restrictions on foul language. "That bastard tried to take my finger!" Crawdads were always vicious prey

227

to Larry. These hunts were battles worth winning.

Larry dropped the creature into his jar, placed the jar on the ground, then lowered himself into what looked like the beginning of a push-up . . . and stared at his foil. To the crawdad's credit, it turned away.

"Tried to take my finger! Well, he's done."

We never actually killed the crawdads. It was about the hunt. And seeing how many would fit together in a one-gallon pickle jar.

The key to *not* getting a finger pinched — and a crawdad pincer doesn't draw blood — is not reaching under a rock in pursuit of a catch. If you can't lift the rock — surprise, you sumbitch! — you move on to a different, more accessible crawdad cranny.

"This one's small, but fiery." Most crawdads will submit once removed from the water. But now and then, one put up a fight, flailing its tail and pincers in a slimy jig that made the transition to the pickle jar the hardest part of the endeavor.

"Dammit!" I dropped him.

"Pick him up, Trey! You catch crawdaddies like you catch baseballs!" Larry had that grin that all but closed his eyes in a devious squint.

Plop. Into my jar Dancing Jimmy went.

And so the hunt proceeded for the better part of

an hour. As always, we found ourselves next to each other in that push-up position, staring at our jars, each with six to ten crustaceans measuring from three to six inches. Six to ten crustaceans that had to be wishing they could be, oh, six feet long for just five minutes. *Wouldn't that be a feast, fellas?*

It was staring at these improvised traps that somehow spurred the deepest conversations Larry Blackwell and I had. I never told Larry about Arline's kiss, but every trip we took down to Crawdad Creek, I *thought* about telling him.

Just as I thought about telling Devon when we rode our bikes after supper. But I kept it to myself. Maybe it was because Arline was a little girl in our world, not even able to call herself a teenager yet. Or maybe by not telling Larry and Devon, I kept that kiss all to myself. Sort of wrapped up nice and tight, in a part of my mind I could visit when the moment was needed.

Larry wasn't nearly as sentimental.

"I think Wendy's boobs have grown since the end of school."

"When have you been close enough to Wendy to measure the size of her tits?"

The thought of Larry so much as catching a glimpse of Wendy was bothersome. Well, it was repugnant.

"I've been close enough. I can see. I know you can see. They've grown."

"Have you ever talked to her, Larry?"

"To Wendy?"

"No, your mom." Cliché. Too easy. First mom insult of the afternoon. And a weak one.

"I've talked to Wendy."

"About what, Larry?"

There was a pause. Longer pause than usual. I turned to look at Larry. He was just staring at the jars.

"Her boobs." And back came that grin.

I resisted the urge to dump my jar of poor-man's lobsters on Larry's back. Would have been an ugly clean-up.

"She's smart. You know that? Wendy's smart." What kind of point was I making?

"Who the hell cares?" Larry sat up and crossed his legs, Indian style. As if we were formalizing the discussion.

"Whether it's me looking at Wendy Nickerson or you looking at Wendy Nickerson, it ain't for her brains, Trey. And you know it."

He was right. But not a hundred-percent right.

"She can throw a baseball better than you, Larry. She can definitely shoot a basketball better than you."

Larry actually leaned back and laughed. Like the villains do in B movies. That enormous mole under his right ear had never been more evident.

"You've got a crush on a jock! Admit it, Trey. You want to hump a baseball player!"

We'd landed in crude-ville. Your captain in the cockpit: Larry Blackwell.

"I don't have a crush on Wendy." Lying to myself?

"You want to hump a baseball player, Milligan."

"You know, Larry. I have talked to Wendy. And not about her boobs. She's a nice person. She laughs easily. I don't feel nervous around her." Another lie.

"We have some things in common," I continued. "It's cool to hang out with a girl who can make a jump shot, or play catch without wincing every time you throw her the ball. And yeah, she's pretty." Truth's out. "Fantasize all you want, Larry. I think Wendy's cool."

Larry just grinned at me. And stared.

I picked up my jar — eight crawdads at last count — and took it over to the creek's edge. Tipped it over and let the gang back in. Back home.

Then I walked back to where Larry was still sitting, now stirring his own jar with a stick, agitating the crawdads. Always agitating, Larry.

"Remember Devon's funeral?" I asked the

231

question not so much literally, but to set a place and time.

Larry kept stirring his jar. Without looking up, he said, "Yeah."

"I sat next to Wendy. She was wearing a purple dress." The image is one I've never let go . . . and never will.

Now Larry looked up. Even took the stick out of his jar. "I remember, Trey. What, you fell in love at a kid's funeral?"

My agitating friend may have, for once in his life, been dead on. But that was not my line of discussion.

"Wendy had bruises on her wrist. Both wrists. Seemed strange. I saw her a few days ago, and they were still visible. Lighter, but still visible."

Larry crinkled his mouth to one side, drew his head back. "She's playing ball all the time, Trey. You said so yourself. Athletes get bruises."

"Bruises on both wrists? At the same time? She can't *dunk* a basketball, Larry."

"Who knows?" Larry got up, took his jar to the creek's edge, and dumped his catch back into the trickling water. Unceremoniously. "You're worried about her wrists? You must be in love with a jock, Trey."

"Just seemed strange. That's all."

Then the day took a turn for the worse. Decidedly.

26

"Check it out." Larry reached into his pocket and pulled out a box of Diamond kitchen matches. Just like the box Gran kept next to her stove. What the hell?

"What the hell, Larry? Are those Gran's?" Had this kid actually lifted a box of matches from my grandmother's kitchen?

"She won't miss 'em." Yes she would. The next time she wants to light a cigarette while drying dishes. What an idiot.

"You took Gran's matches, Larry?" As I asked the question for which I'd already confirmed the answer, my heart rate took a noticeable jump. Matches — and the fire they can create — were not a good fit for Larry Blackwell.

Firecrackers were never enough for Larry. The kids at Cleveland High trafficked bottle rockets like big-city kids moved narcotics. They were too easy to find, especially near the end of the school year, with the Fourth of July approaching. Lighting bottle rockets had become boring to Larry. He preferred to simply sit on the back of his mom's Caddy at the big fairgrounds show. But something about the explosions kindled something in Larry's wandering mind. He liked flames.

The first summer I'd spent with Gran — two years ago — Larry kept a lighter in his pocket. I'd never seen a cigarette near his mouth, but Larry kept that lighter nearby all summer. He'd take it out and strike a flame to kill time. To fill the extended silence of so many summer conversations. And he'd stare at the little flame as it danced above the slim, blue lighter that held its fuel. Stared a little too long, if you ask me.

Last summer, the lighter had disappeared. But not Larry's sense of wonder in staring at a slow burn. One afternoon, with his dad at work (as usual) and his mom at the grocery (not so usual), Larry had presented an experiment in his driveway, one he'd apparently considered and planned specifically for my entertainment.

He stacked newspapers about a foot high, then stacked magazines the same height, about three feet away. Giving me one match — from his mom's stash of matchbooks — and taking one for himself, Larry had us light the two stacks from the bottom, at precisely the same time. To see which stack would turn to ash first. (The newspapers, by a comfortable margin of minutes.)

When his mom came home and saw two charred

spots on her driveway, she demanded what we'd done. Larry told her. Mrs. Blackwell said, "For Pete's sake, Larry!" And that was it.

Which, somehow brings us to our last afternoon at Crawdad Creek.

* * *

"Fire shooter!" Larry held a match against the side of the box — Gran's box — and with a violent thrust of his forefinger, slid the match against the box and into the air. The newly lit micro-rocket charted a low arc before descending into the grass. Yes, the grass.

Larry bounded the seven or eight feet his weapon had flown and quickly stomped out the small fire that weapon had started. He turned back and looked at me with precisely the look you see on a 13-year-old when he scores his first touchdown for the football team. That smile. That glee. "Was that not awesome?!"

"Kamikaze!" He did it again, this time a little closer to my feet than was comfortable. Bounding over to rescue us from his own self-destructive instincts, Larry Blackwell stomped out another little fire. I watched. Heart-rate rising. But silent.

"Japs approaching Pearl Harbor!" Quick thrust, shallow arc, small flame, bounding Larry Blackwell.

"C'mon, Larry. Give me the matches. Someone's

gonna see us." I looked through the ring of pine trees that partially hid the clearing and could see the plastic swingset of the backyard nearest Crawdad Creek. And I could see the houses that lined that street, all too close to kids, literally, playing with fire.

"You're the rescue unit, Trey. Fire shooter!" A match flew toward me again and landed about five feet from where I stood. But this time, there was no bounding Larry. He stood where he'd shot the flame. Still. Smiling at me.

I took the two steps I needed to get to the "landing site," and stomped out the flame. I felt sweat break on my brow. And not the good kind of sweat. Not a pitcher's sweat on the mound. This was the sweat of fear.

"What the hell, Larry?! I'm not kidding. Give me the matches. You're gonna burn this place down." I looked again at that red-and-yellow plastic swingset. And I became, for the first time in my 13 years, genuinely afraid.

I was prepared to make this physical, to take the weapon away from the assailant as they did in the cop shows. But another match was in the air before I could take a step toward Larry. "Fire shooter!"

Again, I hopped to the hot spot, stomped out the flame, and looked up at Larry. Still smiling, he sent another match into the air, this one a bit further for me to pursue. But I got it out. Sneakers, don't fail me now.

I looked up again, and Larry was still. He was smiling at me — this is where I learned what a "shit-eating grin" was — but he was still. Nothing flying toward me. Game over?

I had missed his last shot. Behind me and to my right, in grass taller than where I now stood. This was no "landing site." I sprinted into the grass, but my stomping, this time, only seemed to move the burning grass into more tall, dry grass. As fast as those newspapers had burned in Larry's driveway, they were nothing, it turns out, like dry grass to a flame. I stomped and stomped, performing a dance of panic and fear that had to look funny were a pyromaniac not responsible for the tune.

"God dammit, Larry!! Look what you've done!!"

Out of breath, I stepped back from the growing flame.

This little field was on fire.

I thought I knew panic. Thought I knew paralyzing fear, the kind that locks your brain inside a sound-proof chamber.

There was the time at the beach when I was six years old and drifted too far from the shore courtesy of an undertow. Mom was never out of sight and reached me with a blow-up raft. I was enjoying an ice cream cone within an hour.

There was the first time a fly ball was hit my way in a Little League game. I backed up instinctively (who doesn't?), only to see that ball land ten feet in front of where I'd been standing. The kid got a double and scored later in the inning, but my team — the Padres — won the game. I was eating pepperoni pizza not two hours after the "panic attack."

But this field was on fire. I had started a fire in this field, right next to a neighborhood. Right next to backyard playsets. Larry had helped, to be sure. But I'd set a fire, one that was now deciding where and how to destroy whatever it could. And how fast.

I looked at Larry, but he didn't look back at me. He was staring downward, at the growing flames. He seemed to be wobbling left to right (dancing with the flames?), but maybe that was the blur of panic in my eyes. Worst of all was what I saw on Larry's face. He was grinning. Like me, he was beading with sweat from the heat (and panic), but he was grinning. I wasn't.

"Larry!"

He continued to stare. Continued to wobble.

"Larry!! We've got to put this out!!"

I thought of the pickle jars.

"Get the jars! Get water! Larry!!"

Staring. Wobbling. Still.

I actually stomped at the flames nearest my feet, but did so as I backed up, the flames seizing territory I had to concede for self-preservation. Smoke was thickening, but I could see Larry. He was starting to back up — toward the creek — but wouldn't take his eyes off the flames. Wouldn't stop staring at his creation. At my creation. At *our* creation. He never said a word.

My mouth felt like chalk. My heart was beating like the pistons of a stock car engine. I could breathe, but only because I had to. As I continued to back up — nearer the creek, the same direction Larry was going — I saw the flames marching the other direction, too. Toward that backyard swingset. Toward those houses. Toward a neighborhood.

"Larrrrry!!!"

As I screamed his name, Larry Blackwell turned toward the woods . . . and ran. He jumped across a narrow section of the creek and disappeared into the wooded hillside, climbing toward . . . home? Was Larry running home? He had to be. Get to Larry's house, call 911, and save what we could before an entire neighborhood was incinerated.

I turned and ran. My leap across the creek fell short, my right foot splashing into the water. (It had never felt so cold.) Maybe I crushed a crawdad on that leap. But I didn't break stride, didn't so much as stumble. The pistons beating inside my chest, I broke the tree line and started climbing the hill (it had never seemed so steep) toward Larry's house. Toward salvation. Toward rescue?

27

I'll never forget the silence. Has to be an element of panic, that mental lock-down where your brain is giving you what you need to survive — the muscle power to sprint up a wooded hill for instance — and the rest goes blank.

Every stride I took, I could feel the dried, long-dead leaves crunching under my sneakers. But I never heard the crunch that came with it. While I could feel my lungs starting to burn — that word — I couldn't hear my rapid breathing, not like I would on a jog or a basketball court. Silence. Horrifying silence.

Halfway up the hill, I stopped. Where was Larry? I could see the break in the tree line ahead of me. Above me. There's no way he got up this hill that fast. I could lap Larry in a 400-yard race. I'd seen him try and sprint, rare occasions when he tried to keep up with Devon and me on our bikes. It was an awkward sight. Where the hell was he? My chest heaved in and out as I looked left and right.

I resumed the hill-climb.

Finally at the tree line, now bathed in sweat and the smoky grime from my self-made inferno, I paused long enough to orient myself, to locate

Larry's house, not 100 yards to my right, across the street. (What would a driver have thought had he passed me at just that moment? I had to have looked like an escapee from hell. Which, I guess you could say, I was. Or hoped to be.)

At first I only saw the Blackwell house. (Where the hell was Larry?) There was a kind of relief, as there is with any destination reached. One more sprint and I'd have access to Larry's mom, at the least, but certainly a telephone. My first 911 dial.

Then I saw the red pickup. It's rear was facing me, still in the right lane, but right in front of Larry's house. And I could tell the driver was inside, behind the wheel. This was more than a kind of relief. It was the real deal.

I screamed, "Herb!!!!" And I raced toward Herb Wilbury's truck.

My cousin/uncle/savior turned to look at me as I sprinted to his window, and I saw the look that would have been on a driver's face had he passed just as I came out of those trees. Herb had told me stories of catching snakes with his teeth and arm-wrestling men on death row. And Herb looked absolutely petrified.

"What in holy, hell?! Trey!!"

My throat tightened. Was I going to cry? Not now. No way.

"Trey!! What happened? Where have you been?!"

I took the deepest breath I took that entire summer. My throat relaxed. My chest still heaved. In and out. In and out.

"Herb. We messed up. There's a fire. A big one. Down at Crawdad Creek. I didn't mean to, Herb!"

"Get in the truck, boy! Now!!"

I sprinted around the front of the truck, got in, and pulled the door shut as Herb wheeled his pickup around, almost clipping the Blackwell mailbox. As he hit the gas, taking us back down the hill — via asphalt this time — I looked back at the Blackwell house. Where the hell was Larry?

* * *

Herb knew where he was going. He leaned over the steering wheel, as though leaning would get him there faster. It's the most serious I ever saw Herb Wilbury. No jokes, no sarcasm, no sound really. His eyes were piercing the road ahead as he drove us toward a calamity of my causing.

I sat silently. And I stared at him in admiration. I didn't know what we were going to do. Didn't know if I'd even survive what we were going to do. But I knew Herb had a plan. I could see it in those slits. In those eyes.

We got to the stop sign that met the two-lane

244

highway adjacent to Gran's neighborhood. And I saw the smoke for the first time. Above the one-story homes to our left, maybe 500 yards away. It looked to be a distance away, somehow. But I knew where that smoke came from. And I remembered a standby line of Herb's fantastical storytelling: "Where there's smoke, Trey, there's always a flame or two."

Herb turned left on the highway. He actually drew some rubber in making the turn. Then he turned left onto Chester Lane. We were heading straight toward the fire.

I could see people outside, in front of their homes. All of them looking at the same thing I was. Unlike me — and Herb — they were all wondering, *what started this fire?* There were kids. Girls holding dolls. Boys with toy trucks or action figures. (Did that kid have a fire truck? Perfect.)

We finally reached the street's dead end, just past the house with that playset in the back yard. The one I'd noticed when Larry and I were merely staring at captured crawdads in our pickle jars. And now, Herb and I had a front-row seat at the hottest show Cleveland would see in 1982.

The flames weren't high. The grass was tall enough to serve the hungry flames plenty of fuel, but the fire was spreading outward, not upward (yet). We'd been lucky — could I still use that word for

Larry and me? — in that the clearing had allowed the flames to crawl without finding trees. Trouble was, the flames were crawling toward *homes*. And they were crawling *fast*.

Two men were spraying fire extinguishers. One heavyset and shirtless, the other balding, with jeans and an Atlanta Falcons t-shirt. They attacked the flaming monster from the side closest to the homes. But they were armed with extinguishers built for tiny house fires, a grease fire in the kitchen maybe. They may as well have been jabbing at the knees of a grizzly bear with a yard stick.

Still frozen in my seat, I caught Herb in my peripheral vision. He'd raced to the back of the truck and was pulling blankets over the side. Horse blankets. Tossing them to the ground.

"Trey! Get out and grab one, boy!!"

I looked into Herb's eyes and saw the fear. Which only scared me more.

"Trey!!!"

His shout shook me alert. I opened the door and grabbed the blankets Herb had thrown to the ground. By the time I looked up, he was racing toward the monster, toward the two heroes already fighting the killer I'd brought to life.

Without saying a word, the heavyset fire-fighter tossed his extinguisher aside and grabbed one side of the blanket Herb offered him. The two men then, with the synchronicity of ballet dancers, flung the heavy cloth over as much fire as it would cover.

The duo unfurled another blanket and did the same. I was close enough now to hear them grunting with effort. Close enough to feel the intense heat a field afire creates. I handed Herb one of the blankets in my arms and watched the routine a third time.

And that's when I heard the sirens.

Fear can be both friend and foe. When it keeps you away from the edge of a cliff on a mountain hike, fear is your best friend. When it freezes your mind and body — locks you up inside, turning you into a flesh-and-blood mannequin — fear is your worst enemy.

When that fire truck turned toward me — toward us, toward the flames — I became frozen with fear. An already dangerous situation now became one where an authority (firemen) would be interested in the *cause* of that dangerous situation. That cause stood as stiff as a fence post, staring at the approaching truck. Holding one last blanket . . . until the man in the Falcons shirt ripped it out of my left hand. Stiff. Staring.

There were five of them. Five firemen (counting the driver) emerged from the truck. One, hose in hand, ran across the street and connected the unraveling snake of life to a hydrant, one I hadn't seen until just now. Two of his partners then joined him in racing back toward me — toward the flames — and the three of them together unleashed that hose on the grassfire Larry and I created.

This was power and fury. The power of water pressurized to damage anything in its way. (I remembered images from Mr. Perry's 7th-grade history class of cops turning these hoses on civil-rights protesters during the Sixties. If the water could knock a grown man to the ground, what chance did fire have?)

But the fury of a loose flame gains flexibility when feeding on a field of grass. The firemen sprayed above the flames, letting the water rain down on as large an area as one hose could cover. The three men holding the hose — aiming the hose — worked as though they were born with it in their hands. It moved as smoothly as a giant snake would, the three of them performing a dance — left to right, forward, then back — as though they were listening to the same waltz. It was beautiful. Horrifyingly beautiful.

A hand on my right shoulder.

"Are you okay, son?"

It was the driver of the fire truck. Closely cropped red hair. His eyes as calm as a librarian's.

My mouth agape, I nodded at him. Still frozen in mind, if not body.

"You sure? How'd this happen? Did you see what started the fire?"

Mouth agape. Still frozen.

"Get in the truck, Trey." Herb's voice was an octave lower than the one I'd known for years. He came up from behind me. Covered in sweat, dust and grass clinging to the moisture on his arms and cheeks. His chest was heaving, but he was in control. Reached out and shook hands with the red-headed fireman.

"Get in the truck, Trey. Now."

The flames were gone. That quickly. As I walked toward Herb's truck, I looked back at what was now a water-soaked mess. Charred, black earth, but soaking wet. Smoke still in the air, the threat was gone. Dead. Drowned by eight new heroes.

Three men who woke up this morning thinking a lazy day awaited. And five firemen trained for precisely the kind of day Larry and I had given them. I got in Herb's truck, closed the door, and rolled down the window. It was hot, even without a yard fire in the mix.

The next thirty minutes were among the longest I've lived. A police car arrived with two officers. No sirens. But if the firemen represented authority, what did two cops — each with badges and handguns — bring to this picture? To the picture I'd painted?

The two cops spoke first with the red-headed fireman. (Is the driver of the truck always the boss?) But the fire truck was reloaded and gone as quickly, it seemed, as it had arrived.

The police officers then spoke with Herb. And the guy in the Falcons shirt. And the heavy guy. The heavy hero. They were out of earshot. One of the officers — he was thin, with blond curls escaping the bottom of his hat — took notes, while his partner nodded throughout the conversation. At one point, the blond cop paused and turned toward me. Long enough to make eye contact through the window. Busted. Finally busted.

There were still people outside their homes, on the sidewalk, watching. Behind me, behind Herb's truck. Cleveland was a sleepy town, maybe. But fire trucks and police cars mean show time, wherever you live. I wanted to disappear. Or rewind one day of my life. Just one.

Today would have been a good day for comic books. And I had a stack of Spider-Man comics in my room at Gran's. Stories about a hero. And bad guys. Bad guys that always got caught.

Herb shook hands with both cops. He picked up his horse blankets, now soaking wet, and threw them in the back of the truck. He got in, pulled the door closed, and started the engine. We both stared ahead silently the entire drive back to Gran's house. Seemed much longer than it was.

28

Herb pulled into Gran's driveway, right up to the rear bumper of Gran's Buick as it sat in the cool shade of her carport. He turned off the engine and, without looking at me, said, "Stay here." I stayed.

Herb got out of the car and walked through the carport to Gran's door. He opened the door without knocking (he never did that), and went inside.

That's when the tears came. My throat tightened, my eyes burned, and my breaths came in short, violent heaves. *What the hell had I done? What the hell had Larry and I done?*

An uncle who loved me was inside my grandmother's house telling another person who loved me even more . . . that her grandson is an arsonist. That he's sitting outside in the truck, on his way to prison, hell, or worse. The "worse"? Explaining this to my parents, long-distance.

"Hi, Mom . . . Yeah, I'm fine. I love you, too . . . Yeah, Libby's fine . . . Well, Mom, you see Larry and I had an accident. . . . No, Larry's fine . . . Well, you see . . ."

Chest heaving. Tears running down my cheeks now. I found myself praying that Wendy didn't ride her bike by Gran's house at this precise moment. And for the first time since Devon's funeral, I was glad he couldn't be with me. What the hell would Devon say? He wouldn't joke about this. Not the way he felt about Larry Blackwell.

"Trey . . . you did what?! Shit, man. Shiiiiiiiiiiiit."

I caught my breath and the tears slowed. (Had I run out? Can you run out of tears?) My focus shifted — slightly — toward Herb and Gran. I didn't have my watch on, but at least ten minutes passed. Fifteen? I was as low as I'd ever felt, as miserable and nervous and scared as I'd ever been. Yet I still dreaded seeing Gran, knowing what she'd know by the time I saw her again.

The question dawned on me: *Are we most scared by our past, our present, or trauma yet to come?* Ebenezer Scrooge had it easy. Christmas morning cures everything. Tomorrow morning would be August 9th, about as meaningless a date as there was on the Roman calendar. No spirits to visit me tonight, certainly none to absolve me of my misdeeds come morning. I was scared of my future. A thought I'd never harbored before this very moment.

Herb emerged from the house. I wiped the tears from my face with my sweaty hands, human salt water combined with soot and lingering blades of grass for a perfect concoction of juvenile delinquent grime. He walked up to the driver side of the truck and leaned in the open window, but only long enough to say, "Let's go."

I opened my door, got out, and followed Herb inside the house I'd left so innocently less than two hours ago.

The last time I'd seen Gran cry — well, the last time before Devon's funeral — was three years earlier, at Granddaddy's funeral. There's an empathetic pain in seeing your mother — or your grandmother — crying. For those who provide the greatest comfort to be so uncomfortable themselves . . . it's painful to witness. To feel.

Gran sat at the kitchen table (the side she took for our card games). She'd clearly been crying, but she was composed, her back as straight as a flagpole. Her eyes were red. Somehow, she managed to smile at me. This only tightened my throat again.

"Sit down, Trey." Herb's voice startled me. The silence and Gran's smile had started to comfort my ache.

I sat down across from Gran (the side I took for our card games). Herb sat down next to Gran, on her left. One chair was left empty, to my right.

"Libby's in her room, Trey. Herb told her we had some grown-up talk, that she needed to play privately for a while."

My sister. Damn, I really wanted to see my sister. The shocks I'd taken to my system had placed me on some kind of island of egotistical misery, one where only I could be hurting from my little fire party. Libby would hurt, too. And she'd have an even harder time understanding this mess. But she'd be with me. If not immediately — *"What did you do, Trey?!"* — then eventually.

"Gran, I'm sorry. You don't know how sorry I am. I didn't mean to hurt anyone. Didn't want to hurt anyone."

The words came stumbling out, as if sentences and attempts at explanation were fleeing . . . a fire.

"We were just catching crawdads. That's all. Hanging out. Then Larry . . . ."

I paused. Did they know Larry was involved? What am I supposed to say? How much am I supposed to say?

"We know Larry was with you, Trey." Herb glanced at Gran as he said this. Back at me. Then another glance at Gran.

"Trey, listen to me," said Gran. "A police officer will be here soon to talk with you. To ask you some questions."

My heart started pounding. Again. My throat tightened. Again. Of course the police would be here.

"If you've ever taken advice from me, Trey,

please take it now." Gran reached across the table and opened her right hand. I extended my left and took her hand in mine.

"You must tell the truth. About this entire episode, whether or not crawdads are involved. You must certainly tell the truth about Larry being there with you."

"Trey," said Herb, "most likely, those cops are talking with Larry's folks right now. Larry, too."

First of all, Mr. Blackwell would still be at work in Chattanooga. And Larry? *Where the hell was he?* I still didn't know . . . and found myself desperately wanting to know. Now Larry's mom would be home. Maybe she was having a chat with those two cops right now. I didn't mind the image.

"You must tell the truth," reiterated my grandmother. "Lying will make what is already an ugly situation much uglier. You don't want that. I don't want that."

I stared down at the table. Was I going to protect Larry Blackwell? I knew the word *rat*. And I knew it didn't always mean a furry rodent.

"Trey, did you take my matches?"

If there was a case-winning question — and I'd seen a few on *Perry Mason* reruns in this very house — Gran had just asked it.

How long had Gran known her matches were

missing? Even I hadn't noticed they were missing, and Larry hadn't been here in over a week. She hadn't asked me about them. Libby wasn't tall enough to reach the shelf above the stove, where Gran kept the matches. How long had Gran known they were missing?

Herb stared at me, his brow furrowed in a way I'd never seen before. Gran stared, too. But no furrowed brow.

"Did you take my matches, Trey?"

Still staring at the table, I decided to go with the truth: "No."

"Did Larry have my matches? Were the matches you had today mine?"

Sticking with the truth: "Yes."

I was done crying. And while I wasn't going to blame Larry Blackwell entirely for the mess I'd helped create, he would be part of the story. Part of the truth.

"I didn't know he had them until today, Gran. I swear. He took them out at Crawdad Creek. Last time I saw them they were on your counter. Here in the kitchen."

Gran's eyes were glistening, but she didn't blink as she stared at me. Herb had his hands clasped together on the table. He was staring at them when the doorbell rang.

257

Herb got up and walked across the kitchen to open the door as my heart rate (yet again) picked up its pace.

"Jeff." Herb greeted our guest by his first name, one I didn't recognize. Then "Jeff" walked into the house.

"Good afternoon." It was the police officer with the blond hair. The younger one. He didn't have his hat on now. And no partner followed him into Gran's house. He was carrying a clipboard. And I'd never seen a badge look so shiny. Set against his dark blue uniform, that badge seemed to be pointing its glare at me. Accusing. Kind of like Gran's wet eyes. I didn't take my eyes off "Jeff's" face.

"Good afternoon, officer." Gran stayed seated.

"I know you'd rather I not be here, ma'am. Sorry to trouble you. My name's Jeff Linden." He crossed the room to shake Gran's hand.

"I'm Will Cooper Johnson, officer. And this is my grandson, Charles Michael Milligan. Please call him Trey."

Officer Linden held out his hand. I shook it. He held my right hand firmly, and noticeably longer than I expected. I kept my eyes up, looking at his, my mouth now as dry as cotton.

"Would you like a glass of water, Jeff?" On cue, my cousin Herb.

"That would be great, Herb. Thanks."

"Could I get one, too?" Dry as cotton.

"Do you mind if I sit down?" The police officer grabbed the back of the chair where Herb had been sitting, between Gran and me (still on opposite sides of the table; I wished I could sit next to her now).

"Please do," said Gran.

Herb placed two glasses of water on the table, walked back to the sink and leaned against the counter, his arms folded. His buddy Jeff sat down, placed the clipboard on the table — I could now see a blank sheet of lined, yellow paper — and took out a pen from his chest pocket, not far from that accusing badge.

"Ms. Johnson, Trey has not been charged with a crime. At least not yet. I'll be asking him some questions, primarily for background purposes. As Trey is a juvenile, a parent or guardian must be present for these questions. Are you comfortable being here?"

"I wouldn't call it comfortable, officer. But I'll be here."

"Would you like an attorney present?"

Gran looked over at Herb. He didn't nod, shake his head, anything. Stared back at her.

"Go ahead and ask the questions, officer. My grandson is an honest boy. He'll tell you the truth.

Please be considerate; that's all I ask."

"Yes ma'am."

Jeff Linden may be asking me questions. Interrogation, they call it. But I'd be answering them for my grandmother.

"Trey, why don't you tell me what happened in that field."

I took a sip of water. Not a big one.

"We were catching crawdads in the creek. We do it all the time."

"We?"

The first word I uttered in my first criminal interrogation, and I was already busted for having an accomplice. A career in crime was not in my future. I looked at Gran, then at Herb. Then back to Jeff Linden.

"Tell him who was with you, Trey," said Herb. It wasn't a question.

"I was catching crawdads with Larry Blackwell."

Linden wrote Larry's name on his notepad.

"Was anyone else with you?"

I shook my head.

"You were catching crawdads. No fire needed for that, right?"

Shook my head again. I looked down at the table, but only briefly. I could hear my dad's voice in my ear: "Like a man, Trey."

"How did the field catch on fire, Trey?"

"We had some matches. And we were shooting them at each other's feet."

"Shooting them? Shooting matches?"

I made a motion with my hands, showing officer Linden how we'd slide a match against the box, with enough force for it to fly several feet after lighting.

"Were you doing this on purpose? To light the field on fire?"

"No . . . not at all. We were goofing around. Larry would shoot one at me, and I'd stomp it out."

"Larry shot the matches at you, and you put them out with your feet."

"That's right."

"Obviously, there was a match or two you weren't able to extinguish."

Looked down at the table. And back up.

"That's right."

"Let me ask you this, Trey: Did you shoot matches at Larry's feet?"

How do I answer this? I looked down, then up at Gran. ("My grandson's an honest boy. He'll tell you the truth.")

"Trey, did you shoot matches at Larry's feet?"

"No I didn't."

The police officer began writing on his notepad. Sentences, it appeared. Descriptions. Was I being quoted? Was I "on the record"?

I looked up at Gran, who looked back at me, more with compassion in her eyes than shame. I looked at Herb, standing next to the sink. He had his arms folded, and was staring at his work boots. Inside my chest, anxiety began dancing with fear. What I would pay to start this day over again.

Linden stopped writing and looked up at me again.

"Tell me about how the fire spread, Trey."

I looked at Gran. She didn't say a word; just nodded at me.

"It just happened. I tried to put out the matches, every one. I swear it. I stomped on them. As much as I could. As quickly as I could."

My mouth had never felt so dry. I could tell my voice was changing. My tongue may as well have been coated in sand.

"It just happened. Maybe the wind. Maybe there were too many."

"Too many matches, Trey? Did Larry shoot the matches faster, more frequently? Was that part of the game?

Game. Holy crap. That's what Larry considered it, surely. A game. And look where we were. Well . . . look where I was.

"It wasn't a game. Not to me, anyway. I was

262

trying to put the matches out. Larry was shooting them. If somehow that's considered a game, I guess I lost."

Officer Linden stared at me. I learned to recognize this as a *pregnant pause*.

"I'd say Larry lost, too, Trey. Big time. The two of you are lucky there wasn't more damage, that the fire didn't reach those homes. No one was hurt. If you really consider what might have happened, you might say you and Larry actually *won*."

"Damn right, officer." The first words Herb had spoken since officer Linden had sat down at the table. And for the first time I thought, *my dad is going to remove me from this world*.

"When did you leave the fire, Trey?" The interrogation resumed.

"I saw it was out of control. I wasn't going to be able to put it out. So I ran up the hill, after Larry."

"After Larry?"

"Yeah, up the hill to Larry's house. That's where I saw Herb."

Linden turned back and looked up at Herb. My cousin met his eyes and nodded. A confirmation. In my favor?

"So Trey . . . Larry ran into the woods — up the hill — before you?"

"Yes."

"At what point did you separate?"

The first question I didn't have a real grip on how to answer. I looked back at Gran. Again, she just nodded at me. *Be honest, Trey.*

"I lost him when he got into the woods. I don't know. I thought he made it home before I got to the top of the hill. Is he not at home?"

"My partner's at the Blackwell residence, Trey. We'll find out soon enough." That conversation Herb had at the scene with the two police officers. He'd told them I was with Larry Blackwell. And he told them where Larry Blackwell lives. If Larry and I were criminals, we quite literally sent smoke signals on how to capture us. Easiest case Sgt. Jeff Linden would have in his career.

After making a few more notes, officer Linden capped his pen and returned it to his chest pocket. He folded his hands together, on top of the notepad.

"Again, Ms. Johnson, Trey . . . no charges have been filed yet. I appreciate your honesty, Trey. We'll see what Larry has to say. Then we'll draw up a case to present the district attorney, and see where this goes. You'll hear from us soon."

"Officer," said Gran, "Trey is visiting for the summer with his little sister. He lives in California and will be going home in three weeks."

"I understand. Let's see how this unfolds. I don't

want to suggest one scenario and have something entirely different happen. I'd make sure Trey stays in Cleveland the next few days."

"We're not going anywhere," said Gran. "Just how bad is this? I know you don't want to speculate, but what's the worst-case scenario for my grandson?"

Officer Linden took a deep breath. Looked at me. Then back at Gran.

"In Tennessee, reckless burning is a class-A misdemeanor. And it's a crime just like it sounds: recklessly setting fire to land or a building that belongs to someone else. And recklessly allowing the fire to spread and damage someone's property."

Gran blinked her eyes, looked at me, and then back at Linden. "And what kind of penalty does a class-A misdemeanor bring?"

"The maximum sentence — if convicted as an adult — is 11 months and 29 days in prison, and a fine of $2,500."

You could hear my grandmother gasp for breath. Herb was now staring at me. And I started hoping my father would, in fact, remove me from this world.

"Now, Trey is a juvenile. He'd be tried as such. Worst-case? He'd go to a juvenile center until he's 21."

Another gasp from Gran.

"But Ms. Johnson" — the officer reached out and held Grans' left hand with his right — "that's worst-case. And hearing what I have from Trey, I don't think this will be a worst-case scenario. He has no criminal history. And the fire did not happen on private property."

Officer Linden looked back at me, still holding Gran's hand. "One more reason you and Larry can actually count yourselves lucky. Had those flames reached so much as the backyard of one of those homes, we have a different situation."

I was 13. The thought of going anywhere until I was 21 may as well have been a life sentence. How could a summer in which my best friend died possibly get worse?

"Thanks for your time, folks. And again, Trey, I appreciate your honesty."

Officer Linden let go of Gran's hand, stood up, shook Herb's hand, and returned his hat to his head. "I'll be in touch, Ms. Johnson. Hopefully by tomorrow."

Gran always walked guests to her door. But not this time. She remained seated at the dining table, hands now in her lap. Herb followed the police officer to the door, and closed it gently after he left.

I looked across the table at my grandmother.

And I started crying. My first tears of shame.

She reached both hands across the table, palms up. I took them in mine. Dropped my head to my chest as the sobs squeezed my throat.

"You should be hurting, Trey. This is dreadful. But you're going to be okay. You were honest. And no one has been hurt, thank the lord. Come over here and hug your grandmom."

I wiped the wetness from my cheeks, walked around the table and hugged Gran. Tightly.

"I'm so, so sorry. I promise I didn't mean for this to happen."

"I know. I know, Trey."

29

I never closed the door to my room at Gran's house. But I did now. Sat on the bed, staring at my desk maybe four feet away. Baseball cards in neat stacks, divided by teams, catchers on top. They'd been a priority of mine this morning, before my rendezvous with Larry and the end of my childhood. Was that just a few hours ago?

A scratching at the door. Three scratches, then a pause. Three more. It was Bootsie. I let her in. Sweet dog, she wasn't used to being on the wrong side of the door. (I didn't answer the scratches when in the bathroom. Which is why the outside of Gran's bathroom door was stripped of its sheen across the bottom, six inches above the floor.)

Bootsie couldn't make the leap to my bed, so I lifted her up and let her lie down next to me. Amazing world, that of a dog. She may have known something was wrong, may have smelled the fear, shame, and sorrow on me. (She certainly smelled the salt of my sweat and tears. And the filth from . . . the fire.) But Bootsie the Boston Terrier had no idea I'd been transformed into an arsonist, a juvenile criminal.

What had Officer Linden called it? A "juvenile center." Juvie. Holy shit. I just wanted to play baseball. I'd play alone in Gran's backyard. For life. Let that be my sentence. But a juvenile center? Juvie? Me?

I heard Gran walk past my door, now closed again. Heard her walk into Libby's room, on the other side of the wall. My grandmother was now going to explain to my little sister that her brother was a criminal. An arsonist.

And my throat closed tight again. Eyes stinging. I had considered Gran being ashamed of me. Knew Mom and Dad would be. (When is that phone call going to happen?) But my little sister ashamed of me? That would be too much.

Bootsie slid her head onto my right leg, as though she needed a pillow. Amazing world, that of a dog. She may have known something was wrong, but she just needed a leg pillow. And a nap next to the boy she loved.

Twenty minutes passed, maybe thirty. And Gran knocked on my door.

"Come in."

She opened the door and was holding Libby's hand.

"Your sister wanted to say something to you, Trey."

Libby stared at me for a moment, her hand still holding Gran's. Blonde pigtails dangling from each side of her 8-year-old head. And from her t-shirt, Strawberry Shortcake seemed to actually be mocking me with an inappropriately large grin.

Libby walked up to me, put her arms around me, and rested her head on my right shoulder, her face turning toward Bootsie, who found herself in the middle of a human hug sandwich.

"I love you, Trey."

Once again, sobs. Couldn't hold it back. Why did this day have to happen?

"You need to clean up, Trey. Take a shower. Get into your pajamas. I'll heat up some meatloaf and okra."

I could set a field on fire, but I wouldn't go to bed without supper. Not at Gran's.

Libby turned and walked toward the door, but I stopped her before she turned down the hall.

"Libby."

Again, that Strawberry Shortcake grin.

"Thank you. You're a great sister."

She smiled. Maybe even bigger than Strawberry Shortcake. And it made me feel good. Until the moment it happened, I wasn't sure that was possible anymore.

I turned the lights out around 9:00, because there

was nothing to do, really. But that included sleeping. Just wasn't going to happen. Darkness may ease most senses, but it quickens the pace of a guilt-ridden mind. The phone rang at 10:12 p.m., according to the red numbers glowing on my digital clock. I know because I was wide-awake.

At 10:19 Gran opened the door — no knock this time — and turned on the lamp next to my bed. Spider-Man comic book next to the lamp, waiting to be read again.

She sat down on the bed and put her left hand on my chest. I blinked my eyes as I looked up at her, adjusting to the invasive light.

"That was Mr. Blackwell, Trey. Larry's home."

Where the hell had Larry been? I never wanted to see the clown again, and I desperately wanted to know . . . *where the hell had he been?*

"Where was he, Gran?"

"Best I understand, Trey, Larry came home after the police officer left the Blackwell house. Mr. Blackwell had a long visit with Officer Linden's partner. He knows what happened. And he knows Larry's role."

He knows Larry's version of Larry's role.

"Did Larry hide from the cops?" Had the little prick hid in the woods while I ran to get help?

"I think that's a safe guess, Trey." Gran tapped

me gently with her left hand. "I think that's a safe guess."

He had hidden in the woods while home-owners, firemen, and police officers — not to mention his friend from California — frantically worked to minimize the damage he'd caused. Then he'd stayed outside — hiding — until the police cruiser finally left his parents' driveway.

"You and Larry need to keep to yourselves a few days." Translation: stay away from the monster, Grandson. Stay away.

"Mr. Blackwell said he'd check in with us once he's had a chance to follow up with Officer Linden."

I suddenly saw the image of Mr. Blackwell smiling on that billboard halfway between Cleveland and Chattanooga. Blackwell, Brownstone, and Crowley. Ready to solve your biggest legal problems. *We're Here For You!*

Gran turned out the light and this time left my door open. Bootsie came in and curled up on the rug next to my dresser. And finally, mercifully, I fell asleep.

* * *

My conversation with Mom the next day wasn't as painful as I thought it might be. Libby's hug had helped me with perspective on family in the face of a crisis. "I love you, Trey."

Gran made the phone call. She felt it best that Mom (or Dad) heard an account of the pyro party from someone other than one of the suspects. (I've learned to love and mock that word when crimes are committed in full view, as mine was. What was there to "suspect" about my role in that fire? Or Larry's, for crying out loud.) I waited in my room until Libby — on Gran's signal — came to get me. This was teamwork. Public relations, really. Gran, my sister, and I were presenting a story . . . fashioned as best we could for my parents to handle three time zones away.

Dad was at the university, so Mom would have to explain things to him when he got home later that day. (More p.r.) But I knew she was speaking for the two of them. And, while angry — and surprised, really, more than any other emotion — Mom was the compassionate force she'd always been.

"You're better than this, Trey. You're so fortunate it didn't turn out worse. Much worse."

My side of the conversation? A series of, "I know, Mom." And, "I'm sorry, Mom."

She advised me, in her words, to "keep some distance between you and Larry the next three weeks." Three weeks from now and I'd be on a plane from Atlanta to Los Angeles. Larry Blackwell had officially been given a summer ban from the Milligan family. Right now, he was the last person I wanted to see. Let this be my punishment.

Four words have stayed with me from that phone conversation with Mom: *"Remember who you are."* She spoke them quietly near the end of our chat, almost in a whisper. *Remember who you are.* Our identities matter, it occurred to me, and our identities are shaped by the choices we make. And by the actions we take. I was Trey Milligan when I found myself in the middle of a fire set with Larry Blackwell. And I'd be Trey Milligan through the aftermath, and well beyond. Would "pyromaniac" be part of *who I am*? Hell no.

Later that night, Mom called back. She and Dad had decided on my punishment. (My dream of the Larry ban being enough was just that.) Dad had initially insisted I write an essay on what I'd done — and how ashamed I was — and send it to the *Cleveland Daily Banner*.

After further consideration — consideration led by my mother, rest assured — it was decided that might not be the best way to minimize damage from my flame-throwing bash with Larry. So I was to write the essay . . . but address it to my family: to Mom and Dad, to Libby, to Gran, Herb, and Auntie. To the people I love. To the people who love me. *Remember who you are.*

274

I was to have the essay written by the time I arrived home in three weeks. My first assignment, you might say, outside a classroom. And a doozy.

* * *

The week after the fire was the quietest all summer. Too quiet, really. Gran didn't take Libby and me with her to visit Auntie. She clearly wanted to explain to Auntie what had happened, and save me from Auntie's shock (and initial reaction). Really, Gran belonged in public relations.

I got angrier and angrier at Larry, and it wasn't so much for his cowardly hiding in the woods. Not even so much for the act he'd spearheaded. With each day removed, I grew more and more grateful that the fire hadn't been bigger, more devastating. More deadly.

No, I was pissed at Larry for stealing Gran's matches. A guest in my grandmother's home, he'd taken something that wasn't his to take. And the son of a bitch wasn't going to apologize. Looking back to Crawdad Creek, when I'd first recognized his weapon of choice, Larry hadn't so much as paused when I asked him about the theft. The matches were there, next to Gran's oven, available. I made the connection — eternal — between the words *criminal* and *opportunist.*

And Larry wasn't going to apologize to Gran. If

he was, that call would have been made that first week after the fire. Or he would have appeared at Gran's door with his mom or lawyer dad. Doing the right thing. *"I'm sorry for taking your matches, Mrs. Johnson. I have no excuse. I humbly ask for your forgiveness."*

Nope. Larry wasn't going to apologize. And this said as much about his parents as it did about his own shortcomings. I learned a descriptor for Larry's kind — for the Blackwell family kind — not long after that summer came to an end: *common.*

Call me what you will: irresponsible, careless, selfish. Call me cruel, even. But don't ever call me common. Look it up.

* * *

I played solo baseball in Gran's backyard. Hurled that rubber ball against Gran's patio deck harder than ever before. The activity helped those quiet days — after the fire, the days were uncomfortably quiet — move along. There was a form of peace I found under my Cardinal hat. The rhythm of throwing a rubber ball . . . *thwap. Thwap. Thwap.* Always with my fitted Cardinal cap pulled tight to my brow.

I had received my Cardinal cap on our first Christmas morning in California. Dad had gotten me an Angels hat — the kind with the mesh backing and plastic, adjustable strap — thinking it would make me feel closer to our new home. He underestimated my devotion to Lou Brock, Keith Hernandez, and Ted Simmons. And he'd corrected the mistake on Christmas morning. The hat wasn't even wrapped. It was sitting on top of the wrapped gifts, its magnificent logo — "STL" — staring at me as Libby sprinted for her stocking. And it fit perfectly. To this day, I don't know how Dad knew my hat size (7 ¼").

There was peace under that hat. Especially in Gran's backyard. Especially with one friend dead, another essentially under parental house arrest, and two girls on my mind . . . neither with any clarity. *Thwap. Thwap. Thwap.*

Today's opponent: the Montreal Expos. Gary Carter, Andre Dawson, and their young speed demon, Tim Raines. He was no Lou Brock. And he was no match for my fastball today.

Arline stopped by one afternoon — again, across the chain link fence — to ask about the incident.

"It was stupid. I don't know what else to say, Arline. We were stupid."

"Did you burn yourself?"

Her question made me consider an element I really hadn't for four days: neither Larry nor I had the slightest physical scar from our fire dance. At least I assumed Larry didn't. I was the one trying to

277

put the flames out.

"No. I'm fine."

"Does Wendy know?"

This question made my heart sink. And brought the weight of shame back to my shoulders.

I wanted to see Wendy. And the last four days, I'd walked by her house, hoping to find her shooting baskets in her driveway. Each time, no Wendy. And worse, no station wagon in the driveway. Seems like Wendy had mentioned a family vacation coming up. (The Nickersons packed into a massive Pontiac Safari station wagon for their annual trip east to Myrtle Beach.) Wendy was, strangely, the person I most *wanted* to know about what had happened at Crawdad Creek. How do you explain that? But to answer Arline's question . . . .

"No. She doesn't know. I think she's on vacation." And the Nickersons would be gone for two weeks, or at least ten days. *I wanted Wendy to know.*

"Larry's no good, Trey." Wisdom from the young maiden across the fence. The one who's kiss I could still feel on my right cheek.

I turned and slung the ball against the patio, and cleanly fielded the rebounding ground ball.

"I know, Arline." I was in no mood to defend Larry, not even out of some sense of skewed loyalty.

278

("He may be a monster, but he's *my* monster, dammit!")

"I just hope it works out, Trey. It's scary. Are you scared?"

Juvenile hall.

"Yeah. You could say that."

"Is there anything you want me to do?"

Arline Varden was a tender person. I'd known her for three years now, but this was my first — quite late — recognition of this trait. She was tender.

"Thanks, Arline. I'll let you know. Just don't talk about it to a lot of people, you know?" *Remember who I am, Arline.*

"Okay. I'll see ya, Trey." She turned and walked slowly toward the trailer park she called home. Her brown hair was tussled, wind-blown. But it also reflected the sun as she grew smaller in the distance. Arline was tender. And she was also pretty. She'd make someone really happy someday.

I turned back toward the patio, wound up, and fired another strike. As my thoughts returned to Wendy Nickerson.

30

Geraldine never drove by Gran's house. Not directly. There weren't enough kids down this section of Westview Drive. The Nickersons lived nine houses down (almost two full blocks). But Wendy wasn't a regular customer. So what was her ice cream truck doing right outside Gran's house? Loudest I'd ever heard "When the Saints Go Marching In," at least from indoors.

Still sweaty from the baseball game — Cardinals 5, Expos 2 — and with my sweat-soaked Cardinal hat still clinging to my brow, I went out Gran's back door, down the driveway, to see what Geraldine wanted. I didn't have so much as a quarter in my pocket.

She was resting her chin in her right hand, her right elbow leaning on the window ledge where she took orders from kids all summer long. Looked like she would have held that position until midnight if that's how long it took for me to come outside.

"Hey, Geraldine." My hands were in my pockets. I knew this wasn't about ice cream.

"Hey yourself, Trey Milligan." She stood up, leaned back, and seemed to be staring down from

Mount Olympus. Somehow, her jingle — *"When the saints . . ."* — kept the moment from being dreadfully heavy. She clearly knew about the fire. And she was parked here outside my grandmother's house to let me — and Gran, and Gran's neighbors — know she knew.

"Whatchu gonna have?" This wasn't about ice cream. No way.

"I gotta save room for supper." It was no later than three o'clock. Prime ice cream time. But this visit wasn't about ice cream. Geraldine's offer was a formality. And an ice breaker.

"That right? No problem, then. So how you doin'?"

I stared at the images and colors on Geraldine's truck. When was the last time I had an orange Push-Up? And did she ever sell those chocolate bananas?

"I'm okay. I guess." There was the opening she needed. Offered it freely.

"You guess? What's 'at mean? You guess you're okay?"

"Yeah. I guess I'm okay, Geraldine?" Awkward. "How are you?"

"Well, I never *guess* how I'm doin', if that's what you're askin', Trey Milligan."

I turned from the ice cream images and looked up at Geraldine.

"I always know how I'm doin'. There's too much in this world that makes us guess, Trey. Things that make us wonder. Things that confuse us and worry us and confound us. You know what confound means, right?"

I knew what confound means. I nodded at her. Wishing this conversation was about ice cream.

"I heard you and Larry damn near burned the place down."

The place?

"Heard if it weren't for some neighbors, your uncle, a firetruck, and a police officer, I wouldn't have too many customers in these parts anymore."

Herb was my cousin, technically. Did I need to clarify this? Seemed unimportant. I looked down at the Nutty Buddy label, then back up at Geraldine.

"Is that true, Trey? You and Larry set fire to the neighborhood?"

I'd seen that fire spread at my feet, seen how fast it spread. But the speed of that fire was nothing compared with how fast word spread of two kids screwing up. Two . . . *pyromaniacs*. Remember who you are, Trey.

"We didn't set fire to the neighborhood, Geraldine. It was a small field, next to Crawdad Creek. It was scary, but we were lucky and it was put out pretty fast. Could have been a lot worse."

Geraldine cracked a smile for the first time during this visit. Then she placed her hands on the window ledge and leaned down toward me.

"Could have been a lot worse. C'mon, Trey. Who you talkin' to now?"

I found myself wishing Gran would call me inside. Or the skies would open up with rain. Come on, thunder shower.

"How long we known each other, Trey? Three years?"

This was my third summer at Gran's. Geraldine paid attention to details.

"You're on your way, Mr. Cardinal. But you ain't gonna get there with Larry Blackwell at your side."

Back at the Nutty Buddy label. Back at Geraldine.

"You ain't gonna get there with Larry Blackwell, Trey. And since Devon ain't here anymore to tell you so . . . well, that's my job. And I don't mind tellin' you."

I found myself shaking my head slightly, staring at that damn Nutty Buddy label.

"Do you disagree? Trey . . . why you shakin' your head?"

Eyes back to Geraldine, the one and only ice cream vendor I've ever loved.

"No, Geraldine. No, I don't disagree."

"Why you shakin' your head?"

Regret. I was shaking my head out of regret. And wishing she hadn't brought up Devon. Sure didn't help my current situation.

"I don't know, Geraldine. I guess I just regret what happened. And how it happened. And who it happened with. The whole thing. I regret it."

"Damn right, you regret it. And that's what I'm talkin' about, Trey. You're on your way. You know right from wrong. Your mama and daddy do. Your grandmama sure as hell does. Devon did. That pretty little Arline does."

This time, I nodded.

"But Trey . . . Larry Blackwell don't know right from wrong. Worse than that, he seems to *like* wrong. You hear me on this?"

Again, I nodded. Wasn't about to defend Larry now.

"We all have to live the life God gives us, Trey." Geraldine had rarely gotten spiritual with me. Seemed to fit her tone now, though.

"But we have to choose the people we let in, Trey. And every person we let in paves the path with us. You help pave my path, Trey. You're my friend, and I let you in the first time I sold you a Nutty Buddy. I knew. You fit right alongside me on the

284

path I'm living. On the path God gave me to live. But I choose the people I let in very carefully."

She actually leaned outside the window now, lowering her head almost level with mine. Almost.

"Choose the people you let in, Trey. Choose them very carefully. They'll help you pave your path. But if you let the wrong kind in . . . if you let the wrong kind start to pave your path with you. Well, ain't no one to blame but yourself. Because you was the one let 'em in."

I nodded. Stared once more at the Nutty Buddy label.

"Here. On the house." Geraldine handed me a Nutty Buddy. The most valuable Nutty Buddy I'd ever receive.

"Thanks, Geraldine." My eyes smiled at her, if my mouth couldn't.

"Tell your grandmama I said hey. And watch out for those Phillies."

She took her seat on the other side of the truck, smiled at me, and put the truck in gear. Before pulling away, she turned off her jingle.

It was the last time I ever saw Geraldine.

31

There are plenty of ways to define *deliverance*. Liberation can be achieved in various forms, by a multitude of methods. For me, deliverance came in the form of a bacon quiche.

It was a Tuesday morning, my last in Cleveland that summer. I'd be catching a plane home to sunny California the next Monday, in Atlanta.

The morning was typical. Two episodes of *Three's Company* with Libby. (Mr. Farley hoodwinked in both that day.) Then baseball in Gran's backyard. Today's opponent: the Houston Astros. (The true-to-life St. Louis Cardinals were in the midst of a streak in which they'd win eight of nine games and take over first place in the National League East from the Philadelphia Phillies.)

I must have been outside an hour and a half, when Gran opened the sliding-glass door to her patio. Lathered in sweat. It was the top of the eighth inning. Doug Bair was pitching in relief for the Cards. Bill Doran was at the plate for Houston. I never finished that game.

"Come inside, Trey."

It wasn't lunchtime. As far as I knew, we weren't

going to see Auntie until our usual Wednesday-afternoon visit. Gran never interrupted my baseball games.

Ball secured in my glove, I walked up the patio steps, through the still-open glass door, and into Gran's den. She was sitting on the couch.

I glanced to the other side of the room, into the kitchen. Resting on the stove top was a tan, rectangular dish. Inside that dish, I'd soon learn: a bacon quiche.

I sat down in the swivel chair next to Gran's desk, across the room from her. She clearly had something to say.

"We just had a visitor, Trey."

She just had a visitor. One bearing a quiche apparently. Wait a minute . . . .

"Roy Blackwell stopped by while you were outside. He was kind enough to bring us a bacon quiche."

Gran loved a quiche as prepared by Crystal Blackwell. It was the *only* thing she loved about the Blackwell family.

"Was Larry with him?" Confusion set in. I still hadn't seen Larry since the flame-throwing affair. Not so much as a phone conversation. But now his dad had seen Gran? Bacon quiche in hand?

"No. He came by on his way to his office this

morning. Didn't want to interrupt your game."

Why would L. Roy Blackwell, attorney at law, want to see me, whether or not I was playing baseball?

"Is Larry okay?" I'd learned news from friends' parents wasn't always good. Such news could actually be devastating.

"Larry's fine, Trey. And so are you, my dear." Gran let a slight grin cross her face.

"What's going on, Gran?"

"Trey, you and Larry aren't going to be charged with arson. You're not going to any juvenile hall. And you certainly aren't going to jail."

I could tell, from across the room even, that Gran's eyes were getting moist. And I could feel a relief — *deliverance* — I hadn't felt in my 13 years, and wouldn't feel quite the same way ever again. I swear, I could feel my blood flowing more happily.

"What happened, Gran? That's . . . that's great. What happened? Was it Mr. Blackwell?"

"It was Mr. Blackwell, Trey. He met with the police officers, convinced them this was a first-time mistake by two boys looking for summer adventure. Convinced the police this was an *only-time* mistake. Your record is clean, my love. And so is Larry's."

Power is hard to recognize until it's wielded. My image of Mr. Blackwell was always that smiling face on his billboards. "If they owe you, you owe it to yourself to CALL US." I'm not sure who owed what to whom in the "adventure" Larry and I had in that field next to Crawdad Creek. But it appeared Mr. Blackwell knew how to bring clarity — *deliverance* — to the mess we caused. And with a bacon quiche for my grandmother a part of the package.

"How did he do it, Gran? Was there a fine or anything?"

"He didn't say anything about a fine, Trey. And you know what? I didn't ask for details. Roy Blackwell brought us the best news we'll hear this summer. And he's helped erase a lot of fear and doubt. So just be grateful, Trey. Be as grateful as I am. I'm not prepared to thank the lord for helping my grandson out of an ugly situation. But I sure thanked a powerful lawyer. And I'll be thanking L. Roy Blackwell in my prayers for the rest of my life."

I stood up and walked over to Gran. Sat down beside her on the couch. I grabbed her left hand with my right. We each squeezed as tightly as we could. And we smiled at each other.

It was a good Tuesday morning.

If only the summer of 1982 — at least *my* summer of 1982 — had ended that day. With hindsight, I would have called it a win.

32

The sirens changed everything. At first a mild distraction . . . somewhere in the distance. Then gradually louder, approaching.

You didn't hear sirens in Cleveland, Tennessee. Ever. Not on Friday night. Not on any night.

Libby was already in bed. Gran had her feet up on the couch. Me, I had one leg dangling over the arm of Granddaddy's lounge chair. *Dallas* had been on 10 minutes, maybe 15. That made it around 9:15 that Friday night.

I wasn't looking forward to the flight home four days from now. Back to Mom and Dad. Back to school. Two thousand miles away from my grandmother, from my summer oasis in east Tennessee. I hadn't been sulking through *The Dukes of Hazzard* and the first few confrontations on *Dallas*. But I'd been silent. Then the sirens.

As they neared Gran's house, their wail began to pierce not only the silence, but my thoughts. *Woo-woo-woo-woo-woo*. I sure as hell didn't care what Bobby Ewing had to say anymore.

I felt my heart rate climb as the police cruisers — two of them, one behind the other — drove directly past Gran's house. This wasn't normal. I looked at Gran. She'd straightened up on the couch, lowering her legs to the floor.

No one was speeding down Westview Drive. Even if some careless teenager had been, no way are two police cruisers dispatched for the chase.

Before the sirens were out of earshot . . . another siren. Coming from the same direction as the police cars. But a different sound this time. A different wail. *Weeee-ooooo . . . weeee-ooooo . . . weeee-ooooo.*

An ambulance. Thirteen years were enough life to know the difference between a police siren and that of an ambulance. Again, the siren grew louder as it neared, then passed directly in front of Gran's house. Following the path of those police cruisers.

My palms were now damp. And Gran's brow furrowed in a way it seldom did until this summer. She was worried, which made me worry. She was scared, which made me . . . .

Wendy. I stood out of the chair as the hair on the back of my neck tingled. Those sirens were moving toward Wendy's house. God, let them move past Wendy's house. Way past Wendy's house.

I didn't bother to find shoes (or socks). As I sprinted out Gran's front door into the darkness, I heard her shout behind me . . . "Trey!"

The sun had long set, but Gran's driveway was

291

warm as I sprinted to the street and turned right toward those sirens. Toward Wendy's house. If the asphalt was this hot under darkness, I thought, a person's feet would melt to the bone at noon. Shoes were good. Anything to distract my brain from the fear I felt squeezing my throat and backbone.

The sirens went silent, but the flashing lights — police cruisers blue, ambulance red — made a portion of Terrace Lane look like a rock stage. But suddenly eerily silent. And all three vehicles — the two cruisers and the ambulance — were parked in front of the Nickersons' house, one of the cruisers diagonal to the driveway, blocking any entrance . . . or exit.

As I got closer, I saw a fourth vehicle, parked in the driveway, just as it was on a typical summer night. Jerry's Camaro. And in front of the Camaro, the maroon Plymouth, Mr. Nickerson's car. The Nickersons were home. Getting the attention of police officers and an emergency medical team.

I was out of breath. And couldn't swallow.

As I got close enough to make out a police officer — a woman — at the end of the driveway, I slowed to a walk. And I suddenly became self-conscious of what I was wearing: tan pajama pants and a black Star Wars t-shirt. No way did I belong here. But no way was I leaving.

The officer turned her flashlight on and pointed it toward me. Blinding at first. But I turned away . . . and saw Wendy sitting on the steps of her front porch. Her mom was sitting with her, an arm around her. Was Wendy in a robe?

"What are you doing, kid?" The police officer walked toward me as I froze in place, my feet planted to that warm asphalt in front of the Nickerson house.

"Wendy!" Her name was out of my mouth before I looked back at the cop, before I so much as considered an answer to the lady-cop's inquiry. This wasn't curiosity. It was pure, adrenaline-fueled concern. I was scared out of my wits, and entirely for the girl who was taking my heart one thought at a time. Again, "Wendy!"

"Son, you need to go home." The lady cop had her own concerns.

"Trey?" Her voice.

The cop actually put her right hand on my left shoulder, tenderly, but my eyes never left Wendy, as she stood up — in a white bath robe — and sprinted down her driveway. Into my arms.

I received her in an embrace I didn't anticipate and never envisioned, not in any scenario my imagination may have conceived. It was tight, her arms encircling my neck in a trembling squeeze I never wanted to end. I held her as tightly as my fear would allow — *What the hell is going on?* — and felt her wet hair under my right hand, just under her shoulder blades. I squeezed her even tighter. This was right.

"I'm so glad you're here." She spoke softly, but it could have been a whisper and I would have heard every syllable, her mouth just under my right ear, her chin on my shoulder. She wasn't crying. But she was trembling. What the hell was going on?

"Wendy, are you okay?" She held me, and I held her back.

"It's okay officer. He's a friend. He's fine."

Wendy's mom was right next to us, asking the lady cop to stand down. I noticed the flashlight was now off. The flashing red and blue lights continued. And I heard another familiar voice.

"Trey. Wendy. Good heavens. Are you all right?" Gran.

Wendy held me. And I held her back.

"Debbie, are you okay? What's happened?" Gran approached Mrs. Nickerson.

I could see Debbie Nickerson had been crying. Unlike her daughter or me, she was dressed in clothes for Friday night. She hadn't been lounging, watching *Dallas*.

"Come with me, Ms. Johnson. I'll be fine." Gran

— wearing a full-length, olive-green raincoat over her nightgown, always decent in public — walked with Wendy's mom down the driveway.

Wendy finally released her embrace, pulled back and looked at me. She then turned to her right and I followed her glance. Right into the backseat of the police cruiser parked in front of the Nickersons' mailbox. Right into the eyes of Jerry Nickerson.

There is fear *for* a person and there is fear *of* a person. Rarely do the two mix into just the right cocktail of terror. But as my eyes met those of Jerry Nickerson under the glare of police lights, that cocktail intoxicated me for the first time. One of east Tennessee's finest high school basketball players looked back at me with a blankness I haven't seen since. A blankness I hope I never see again.

Before I could pull away from this mortifying stare, Wendy's front door opened. And three EMTs emerged, struggling to navigate the porch while carrying a stretcher. A person was on that stretcher, covered to the neck by a white blanket, with an oxygen mask over his mouth and nose. The EMTs carefully descended the stairs from the porch to Wendy's front yard, and walked directly to the ambulance. Directly past Wendy and me. Wendy clung to me again, not quite as tightly this time. She and I watched the EMTs pass with their patient.

Carl Nickerson. Wendy's dad was on that stretcher.

33

That Friday night turned to Saturday morning before I found sleep. Once the ambulance left, the police officers asked Mrs. Nickerson a few questions. Then they left too.

Wendy's mom sat with Gran in the Nickerson kitchen for what seemed like a brief visit. And an eternity.

Wendy and I just sat on the steps of her front porch, precisely where I'd seen her sitting with her mom as I arrived a lifetime earlier. We held hands the whole time, her right in my left. We glanced at each other a few times, but mostly stared straight ahead. The conversation went like this:

"Are you all right?"

"Yeah. I'm okay."

"Are you hurt?"

"No."

"Do you want me to leave?"

"No." Thank god she said no.

"What's gonna happen to your dad and brother?"

Silence.

"Did they hurt you?"

Silence.

"Wendy, sweetheart, you better come inside. Get some sleep."

Gran emerged from the front door. Mrs. Nickerson was still inside.

"It's time for us to go home, Trey. Wendy's going to be fine."

We stood up. And there was no goodbye hug. But Wendy squeezed my left hand. Squeezed it until it actually hurt. And she smiled at me. Maybe she would be fine. I smiled back as she released my hand and walked back inside her home.

* * *

By the time we got back to Gran's, I realized my kid sister had been home alone for, what, an hour? Two hours? Bless Libby for sleeping through the wails of those sirens. And bless Gran for her concern (fear?). Libby had learned mom and dad's phone number that summer. Gran had left a note on the kitchen table for Libby to "call home" had she awoke to an empty house.

With memories of the chat with Officer Linden at the kitchen table still fresh, Gran and I sat down for a conversation that made my arson case seem like child's play. Gran told me everything Debbie Nickerson told her.

Mrs. Nickerson was at a friend's house, a

monthly "ladies night." Jerry was out doing what rising seniors do on summer nights, let alone Friday nights. And Wendy took a shower. It started as simply as that. As innocently as that. My guess is Wendy had been shooting hoops after supper — wish she'd invited me — and wanted to shower before going to bed.

Carl Nickerson got into the shower with Wendy.

I didn't know how to react to this. To this day, I don't know how to react. Child or adult, a person recognizes sinister when he sees it. Or hears about it. Carl Nickerson grew horns and scales that night. In my mind, Wendy's father died that night.

What Carl Nickerson hadn't planned on was Jerry Nickerson's boredom. His girlfriend was occupied with other social occasions. His drinking buddies wanted to start at the movies, and nothing good was showing.

So Jerry drove home. And when he got inside that home, he heard shouts from the rear bathroom. Wendy's shouts.

According to Mrs. Nickerson, Jerry busted open the bathroom door, pulled his father out of the shower, and dragged the naked man into the hallway, returning what modicum of privacy he could to his kid sister.

And then Jerry Nickerson proceeded to beat Carl

Nickerson with a fury so profound that Wendy called 911 to save her attacker's life. (Only after calling the police did Wendy call her mom at the friend's house to tell her what had happened.)

The bruises. The bruises on Wendy's wrists. No.

I cried. Gran cried with me. We held each other's hands across the table. Both hands. And we cried for my friend Wendy Nickerson.

I wasn't 13 anymore. Never would be again.

The last time I looked at the clock, it was 2:44 in the morning.

34

The day after I learned Devon had died — just five weeks ago — had been my first experience with "mental fog." There was a numbness to all my senses as I tried to take my mind to the place Devon now occupied. Or at least Devon's soul. And I couldn't get there. Sounds interfered (birds chirping?). Sights (a baseball game on TV?). Smells (Gran's fried okra?). These were distractions, interference as I tried to process Devon's death. As I tried to reach what my mom would later call "a new normal."

This was different. I woke up my last Saturday morning at Gran's knowing the previous night was all too real. Wishing it were merely a nightmare did no good; I had woken up too frequently, scared more sirens would be wailing before dawn.

And unlike the "new normal" of recognizing Devon was no longer alive, I knew Wendy Nickerson was alive. More than likely waking up herself, starting a new Saturday. Birds chirping. Baseball's "Game of the Week" on in a few short hours.

But Wendy's father wasn't at home. Neither was her brother (was he?). Some kind of Saturday in

Wendy's life. In mine. There would be nothing normal about this "new."

Gran took us to see Auntie at Springview. Made some chicken-salad sandwiches that we ate in her room, the curtains pulled to allow the sunshine in. And that sunshine. On this day, it only compounded the fog of my mental state. It just didn't seem like a bright day.

Libby was combing the hair of a doll and Gran left to get a pitcher of tea in the cafeteria when Auntie cut the day's atmosphere in two.

"You need to have lunch with Wendy, Trey."

Gran had told her. I wasn't sure how much detail had been shared, but Gran had told her.

"Did you hear me?"

I stared out Auntie's window, squinting. Not sure why my heart began beating more rapidly.

"Yes." I nodded. I had heard her.

"This is important, Trey. She needs her friends now, especially. She needs tenderness. She needs to smile, maybe even laugh. You can help with that."

Gran walked back into the room. Poured a glass of tea for her frail — but oh, so wise — sister.

"Help with what?," Gran asked.

"I told Trey he needs to have lunch with Wendy Nickerson."

"Oh, sure. I think that's a good idea. What do

302

you think, Trey?"

Gran and Auntie had not only discussed what happened Friday night; they had planned the first steps of recovery.

Still squinting, still gazing out the window. "I'm not sure she'll want to have lunch with me. And I've got to leave Tuesday." Would I see Wendy again before my summer-ending drive to the Atlanta airport?

"You need to invite her to lunch tomorrow, Trey. I know your grandmother would enjoy helping you prepare." This was basically an assignment for Gran: sandwiches for a guest on Sunday afternoon. Gran nodded and smiled at the comment.

I felt lost in that fog. A mix of anger, sorrow, and confusion squeezing any clarity from my thoughts. Until, that is, I considered seeing Wendy again. One more time before leaving. Focus returned. Thoughts turned to the future, if briefly, and left the past behind. If briefly. Maybe this was recovery after all.

"Okay. I guess I'll call her when we get back to Gran's."

"Let me call, Trey." Gran stood up and put her right hand on my left shoulder as I continued to stare — continued to squint — out Auntie's lone window. "I'll make sure it's okay with Debbie. They go to church first thing in the morning."

We said goodbye to Auntie that day. She leaned up from her big pillows as best she could and put her tiny arms around my neck, her coiled, arthritic hands patting my back as we embraced. And I hugged her longer than usual. Probably a little too tightly, though she didn't complain. I was learning how fragile love was. Far more fragile than this powerful woman.

* * *

"She'll be here at one o'clock, Trey. Be dressed and ready."

I was boxing up my baseball cards — organized by team nickname, alphabetically — when Gran leaned into my room with a reminder I hardly needed. It wasn't 10 o'clock Sunday morning but I was already showered and dressed. Already nervous.

I wore a maroon cotton shirt — they're called golf shirts today — and blue jeans. Shorts didn't seem appropriate for Sunday, but I wasn't going to wear the suit I wore to Devon's funeral. This was the opposite of a funeral, right? This was recovery. *I hope Wendy doesn't come in a church dress.*

Gran had cleaned the glass table on the back patio and removed two of the four chairs. This was going to be a picnic for two. When I asked her why she and Libby wouldn't be joining us, she said, "You and Wendy need to visit. We'll stay out of the way." Somehow, I was grateful for this. Uncomfortable, but grateful.

Gran had two plates on the kitchen counter, each with three sandwiches. One plate was ham and cheese, the other chicken salad. She had an unopened bag of Ruffles potato chips. And a pitcher of her homemade tea, made with freshly squeezed lemon juice and orange juice ("Russian tea," she called it). For dessert (still in the fridge): lemon meringue pie.

The digital clock above the stove said 1:02 when the doorbell rang.

Gran leaned back against the counter, in front of the sandwiches. "She's right on time. Answer the door."

Yet again, my heart rate quickened. And I opened the door.

"Hi, Trey."

It was the most beautiful smile I'd ever seen. It wasn't a big smile (Wendy's teeth barely showed), but it was a smile. She was wearing a shirt with a green-and-yellow floral pattern. And white shorts. No church dress. Brown sandals on her feet. Yep, this was recovery.

"Hey." I smiled, too. Mine was big; lots of teeth. "Thanks for coming; come on in."

"Hi, Wendy. You sure look lovely." Gran took

no more than three steps forward and took Wendy into her arms. "So glad you could join us for lunch before Trey heads back home." Gran tilted her head so that her cheek touched the back of Wendy's head, right next to a green barrette that held some of her golden hair behind her left ear.

"Thanks for having me, Ms. Johnson."

"Why don't you two head out back? I'll have everything out in a jiffy. Wendy, would you prefer ham-and-cheese or chicken salad?"

"Chicken salad, please."

"And you, Trey?"

"Chicken salad." Of course.

"Hi, Libby." Wendy walked by my sister in the den. She was watching a *Bewitched* rerun on WTBS.

"Hi, Wendy." Libby didn't look up; she might have missed a nose-twitch from Elizabeth Montgomery.

We slid open the glass door and walked outside onto the faux grass — it really was Astroturf, had to be — of Gran's back patio. The humidity immediately opened my sweat glands, as if they needed a stimulant.

"You know, Trey, this is the first time I've been in your ballpark."

My ballpark?

She recognized my confused pause.

"Isn't this where you play baseball . . . by yourself? It's your ballpark, right?"

I had spent the morning considering how best to break the ice, which topics might help (or hurt) Wendy for this most important date of my life. And she managed the trick herself. We could always talk baseball.

"Oh, yeah. Sure. This is my ballpark. Yeah." I smiled and nodded. If only I could have taken Wendy to a real baseball stadium.

"So how does it work? I see the mound." Wendy looked at the dirt patch I'd worn into Gran's back yard, one that would never see grass again.

"Well, yeah, that's where I pitch from. Against the patio." The patio where we were now standing. Wendy spotted one of the rubber balls, near the pitching patch.

"Show me."

My glove was inside. With my Cardinals hat. Awkward. Could I pitch without them?

"You don't want to play baseball now, do you?"

"Come on, Trey. Show me a pitch. We have time for that."

We walked down the patio steps and over to the dirt I made my own for three summers. I picked up the ball.

"Okay, this tree is my second-baseman." To my

307

left.

"That tree is my third-baseman." To my right.

"The fence is like a fence in any stadium. If the ball clears it . . . home run."

"Let's see it pitcher. I heard your fastball couldn't break glass." Wendy smiled when she said this. *Recovery*.

I stared toward the patio wall — reading my catcher's sign — then wound up, kicked my left leg high, and delivered that fastball. *Thwap*. Right back toward me . . . and intercepted by Wendy Nickerson.

"Runner's trying to make third!" Wendy picked up the ball and hurled it toward the maple tree occupying third base. Direct hit.

"What a brilliant play by Nickerson to take down the lead runner! Inning over!! Braves hold their lead over the Cardinals!"

It was the one and only pitch I ever threw as an Atlanta Brave. And it remains the most memorable pitch of my career.

* * *

"Lunch is served!" Gran came outside, two plates on a tray that she placed on the table. Libby brought out the pitcher of Russian tea.

Wendy skipped one of the patio steps on her way to the table. So I did too. *Recovery*.

Gran filled our glasses with tea, then rested her

left hand on my right shoulder after we each sat down. "Need anything else?"

"This looks great, Ms. Johnson. Thank you." Wendy looked up and smiled. Again.

"Okay, then. Just holler if you need me. Libby's insisting on P.B. and J."

Gran slid the door closed and we were alone. My first lunch date. And that fog was clearing by the minute.

"So you're leaving Tuesday?" Wendy took her first bite.

"Yeah, driving to Atlanta to catch my flight to L.A." I took my first bite.

We were quiet the next few minutes. (Gran made amazing chicken salad.) Mostly looked down at our food. (Gran had added pickles to our plates. Needed color, she would have said.) But now and then we glanced at each other. And smiled. *Recovery.*

"I'm gonna be okay."

The words surprised me in how comforting they were. To me.

"I know you are." Didn't know how to respond. Took a swig of tea to consider.

"Things will be different. For my family, I mean. But I'll be okay. I don't want you to worry."

Having entered my teens earlier that year, I'd started hearing an all-too-common bit of wisdom:

Girls mature earlier than boys. I didn't believe such a notion until this picnic with Wendy.

"What's gonna happen?" Still stumbling among ways to respond.

"My dad won't be living with us. I really don't know what's going to happen with him. Hopefully Jerry's not in too much trouble."

Her brother had pummeled Carl Nickerson. And the man deserved his beating.

"Where is Jerry?" Jail? Juvenile hall? I had no idea.

"He's home. He actually got home late Friday night. Or I guess it was actually Saturday morning. The police took his statement and drove him home. No charges. It's just a matter of how my dad reacts."

"Your dad could file charges?"

"Yeah. But mom doesn't think he will. Not under the circumstances. You know?" She took a sip of tea and looked sideways, toward my ball field.

"Yeah. I guess he's in the hospital?"

Wendy kept looking to her right. "He'll be there a few days, they say." Jerry *pummeled* Carl Nickerson. Wish I could have added a punch. Maybe a dozen. Keep him in that hospital a bit longer.

"I don't feel sorry for him, Wendy." The words just came, unfiltered. She looked back at me. Didn't smile this time. She blinked. Twice. But there would be no tears.

"Me either," she said.

Gran cracked open the sliding glass door, her head leaning outside. "Anyone ready for dessert? Lemon meringue pie."

"That sounds great, Ms. Johnson." A smile returned to Wendy's face. *Toughest girl in four counties*, I could hear Herb saying.

"I'll miss you, Wendy." More words, unfiltered.

"I'll miss you, too, Trey. You're my favorite part of this summer."

Lemon meringue pie never tasted sweeter.

35

Bootsie stared up at me from her favorite nap spot in my room: the ugliest chair in at least three counties. Upholstered in a floral pattern heavy on mustard yellow and pea green, the chair was a relic left behind by one of Gran's siblings, a hideous talisman of familial love. And the perfect place for a Boston Terrier to nap.

I wanted to believe Bootsie knew this was departure day, the end of summer for Libby and me. My suitcase was packed and zipped, resting next to the door. I had my Cardinal hat on, a worn rubber ball in my right hand. I tossed the ball, catching it by watching the ball's reflection in the mirror above my dresser. Any activity at all was better than pondering 8th grade. A schedule. Homework. Exams. Deadlines. And 2,000 miles between me and Wendy.

"Five minutes, young 'uns!" Gran called from her bedroom, an alarm for Libby and me to gather anything going with us and head for the Buick.

I stared at Bootsie. Hadn't spent as much time with her as I had in previous summers. Seems like one trauma after another got in the way. But did Bootsie recognize the trauma? She looked as comfortable in that ugly chair as she had any other year I'd been here. Restful. Peaceful.

Leaving Gran's wasn't "sweet sorrow" as Shakespeare suggested. It was just sorrow. A sense of running out of time. Duties called, time quickened. Those we love go separate ways, sometimes temporarily, sometimes all too permanently.

I missed Devon McGee. Painfully. And I was going to miss the ladies — young and old — who made my summer of 1982 so different from any other I'd live. Karen Dunham. (The thought of her looking in Gran's full-length mirror made me smile, even today.) Geraldine. Flossie. (Another smile at the vision of her mowing grass.)

Arline. I probably should have gone to see Arline yesterday (Monday), my last full day in Cleveland. Or at least called her. But I didn't. She knew my feelings. She saw them after our date at the movie theater, when Wendy bumped into us. She probably saw them the last time she stopped by, across the fence in Gran's backyard. Arline gave me my first kiss. She was my first date. But that was it. She knew it, and I knew it.

I was going to miss Auntie. *Running out of time.* She's the reason Wendy came over for that Sunday picnic. I know she was. So wise. And so beautiful, even as she was being slowly attacked by disease.

Mostly I'd miss Gran. If Cleveland, Tennessee, was my briar patch — that's what Br'er Rabbit would have called it — Gran was my Uncle Remus. She was love, happiness, and comfort, all wrapped in human form. And it felt like we were running out of time.

"You coming?"

Gran stood in the doorway, prettier than I'd ever seen her. Dressed for a road trip to Atlanta. Hair just right. A necklace dangling across her navy-blue blouse. Tan slacks with shoes to match the blouse. Love. Happiness. Comfort.

"I'm ready."

Gran closed the passenger-side back door after buckling Libby. As she got in and started the engine, I stared forward. As she backed out of the driveway, I stared forward. As she gently pressed the gas and the car pulled away, I stared forward.

"Stop the car, Gran."

Wendy was in her driveway, shooting baskets. It wasn't yet 10 o'clock in the morning. Did she always shoot so early?

"Be quick, Trey. You've got a plane to catch."

"What are we doing, Gran? Time to go!" Shut up, Libby.

I got out of the car, and Wendy saw me as she grabbed the basketball after it fell through the net. (Girl could shoot.)

"Hey." I didn't know how to do this kind of goodbye.

"Hey." Did she?

"I'm heading to the airport."

"I know."

She didn't take a step from under the basket, so I walked to her. Stopped close enough to touch her, but not yet.

"I guess I just wanted to say bye one more time, Wendy."

She nodded. And her eyes began to glisten. *Please God, don't let me cry here. Let me get to the car, dammit.*

I opened my arms slightly . . . that universal signal. And Wendy dropped the ball.

I'd call it a slow hug. And it wasn't too tight. It was the hug of friends who'd gone through a bit too much together. But were better for it somehow. Maybe better than friends.

Before I pulled away — *You have a plane to catch* — I gently kissed Wendy Nickerson on her left cheek.

And I took off my Cardinal hat and put it on her head. Too big, it sat slightly crooked, almost covered her eyebrows. She smiled, big, and wiped a tear from her right cheek.

"I'll send you a letter."

She nodded again. "Do that, Trey. I'll write you back."

I got back in Gran's car, and we pulled away. I stared forward, trying to freeze the image of Wendy in her new Cardinal hat. That's the one I wanted to take with me. Had to take with me.

The next 20 minutes (maybe 30) were silent as Gran's Buick found the highway toward Atlanta. Even Libby was quiet. Then Gran turned on her tape player. And Slim Whitman sang to us.

EPILOGUE

"Memory believes before knowing remembers."
— William Faulkner, *Light in August*

I didn't hear from Larry Blackwell for almost 30 years. Not until Facebook entered our lives. At work one Monday morning, I opened my page for a status update and saw a friend request from Larry. Clicked on his avatar and there he was. Hair still black as charcoal, now with gel holding it firm. Shiny smile, that enormous mole still mocking the world from under his right ear. He's now a partner, you guessed it, at Blackwell, Brownstone, and Crowley. Larry Blackwell helping others find justice. Yep. How is it that nepotism seems dangerous in every industry but law?

Uncle Herb was found dead of a heart attack in his barn one morning in August 1995. I'm told he was face down, which has to mean Herb was dead before he hit the floor. (He would have chuckled in describing such a demise.) He had a hay fork in his hand . . . never let go. Taking care of his horses. The man who teased me with the lure of fire water — *"Wanna get drunk, Trey?!"* — didn't have a drop of alcohol in his body.

Mattie Clay Caldwell died at the Springview

Senior Center on September 30, 1983. The last time I saw her was the visit when she urged me to have lunch with Wendy. When I hugged her a little tighter, a little longer than I usually did. Auntie taught me more than I knew to thank her for when I was 13 years old. A boy is never too young to be a gentleman. How you dress reflects how you see yourself more than how others might see you. And Auntie taught me how to properly say goodbye. I miss her desperately.

Gran came to see us in California for three weeks during the summer of 1983. By then I was playing baseball — Babe Ruth League — with actual teammates and opponents. She saw more strikeouts than run-scoring doubles from her grandson, but she never stopped cheering. Hell, Gran had been happy when my Cardinals beat her Braves the previous October for the National League pennant. She was pure love.

Gran died of lung cancer in April 1987. Our visits after the summer of '82 were less frequent, and of shorter duration. We were running out of time, as I'd felt when I was just 13. But the times we had together count in life's ledger. They're as permanent as the sun.

I can't hear Bruce Springsteen's "Born to Run" without thinking of Wendy Nickerson. *Together*

Wendy we can live with the sadness. I haven't seen Wendy since that hug in her driveway. We never exchanged letters, and I'm not going the Facebook route. Not for Wendy. Not long before Gran died, she told me Wendy was going to UT-Chattanooga. Soccer scholarship. Of course. I liked to picture a Cardinal hat hanging somewhere in her dorm room at UTC. But that was a long time ago.

Me? I'm a sportswriter. You may have heard of me, though likely not. If I'm doing my job, you'll remember the men and women in my stories. You might follow me on Twitter. I relish the degree of anonymity I've retained, even with bylines scattered all over the Internet.

I've been married to my true love for 20 years now. Eve's beauty is rivaled only by that of our daughters, Marion and Louise. It's a tribute to Eve — and a commentary on my adoration for her — that she made me forget Wendy Nickerson. Well, almost.

We enjoy every summer as if it were our last.

THE END

ACKNOWLEDGMENTS

A writer craves the company of others who practice the craft. I'm grateful to have spent my professional life at Contemporary Media in Memphis, home to many of the finest writers, anywhere. I especially appreciate the support of Richard Alley and Michael Finger with this book. It's also nice to call your longtime boss a friend, as I do Ken Neill.

Thanks to Megan Cox for bringing Trey and his pals to colorful life on the cover of this volume. So much talent, and still so young.

My late father, Frank Murtaugh Jr., and my mom, Melinda Murtaugh, taught me the central value of kindness, and to pay attention to the stories of others. My sister, Liz, trails me only in years and has been a standard by several measures.

I'm blessed to have lived in different parts of the world, but Northfield, Vermont, is my hometown. My friends from that extraordinary community have shaped me in ways I appreciate more with each passing year. I met my wife, Sharon, there (when I was 13 years old); she's my life's greatest gift. We're the proud parents of two remarkable daughters, Sofia and Elena.

Finally, thank you Grandmom. I miss you.